Ineligible Bachelor

Believe
and you are
halfway there!

Ineligible
Bachelor

Enjoy —
Kathryn Quick

Kathryn Quick

Montlake
Romance

The characters and events portrayed in this book are fictitious. Any similarity to real persons, living or dead, is coincidental and not intended by the author.

Text copyright © 2013 Kathryn Quick

Published by Montlake Romance
P.O. Box 400818
Las Vegas, NV 89140

ISBN-13: 9781612186863
ISBN-10: 1612186866

For Mom, always

PROLOGUE

Freddy McAllister lined up at noseguard on defense and peered across the line of scrimmage. Fourth and goal with ten seconds left in the regional championship game. A touchdown meant a come-from-behind win for the Lake Swannanoa Cherokees. Freddy dug in and vowed not to be the Morristown Cougar who allowed the score.

The Cherokees broke the huddle and lined up in the I-formation. The crowd stood to get a better look. It seemed like everyone in the stands knew who was going to get the ball on the snap.

And so did everyone on the field.

Logan Gabriel.

A tough, compact fourteen-year-old, Logan's teammates called him the Logman because he had a tendency to shout "timber" as he ran. Once he got the ball, he routinely cut down anyone in his way like a tree. The team's leading rusher, and good enough at what he did to have a nickname even at the Pop Warner level of football, Logan oozed confidence in every situation.

But today it would be Freddy's job to make sure he didn't get into the end zone.

The Cherokees' quarterback looked over the Cougar defense. His stare lingered on Freddy before he turned and nodded to Logan, confirmation the play was going right through Freddy for the victory. An unearthly silence preceded his barking out the count and the center snapping the ball cleanly into his hands. In one fluid motion, the quarterback turned and pitched the ball to Logan. Effortlessly, Logan caught the shovel pass and headed right for Freddy.

With a deep breath, Freddy ran at him. Logan tried his patented stutter step, but Freddy had seen it too many times: fake to the left, fake to the right, and then run right. Freddy anticipated Logan's move and lunged at him, grabbing on to his legs with both arms, holding on for dear life.

Then, like a tree, Logan fell forward, hitting the ground with a force that knocked the football out of his hands. A red-jerseyed Cougar pounced on the loose ball just as the clocked ticked off the last second and sealed the victory for the visitors.

As the players on the ground unwound themselves from each other, the celebration began. The moans of the losers and the shouts and high fives of the winners merged into a white-noise roar as someone pulled Freddy up by the back of the jersey.

Logan took out his mouthpiece and nodded. "Nice stop, Fred."

Freddy could see disappointment lying vivid in his eyes. "Sorry, Logan, I couldn't let you in."

"I know, but do me a favor, don't take off your helmet until you get into the locker room."

Too late. Freddy had already unhooked the chin strap and started taking the helmet off by the face mask before Logan had even finished the sentence. The skullcap underneath dislodged, and a cascade of blonde hair fell down Freddy's back to her uniform numbers.

Before she could get it back on, some of her teammates hoisted her up onto their shoulders.

"I hope the papers got a picture of your tackle for the front page!" one shouted.

"Fred-dy! Fred-dy!" The chant began on the field and reached into the stands as her teammates carried her around the perimeter.

Helpless on her perch, Frederika McAllister watched the boy of her dreams kick the ground and walk slump shouldered to the locker room.

So much for him asking her to the eighth grade social.

Chapter One

Rikka McAllister hung up the phone and closed her eyes.

She never read the fine print.

"Wake up, wake up. Please, wake up," she pleaded.

She took a breath and held it as she opened one eye. Living room. Darn. She had hoped she would wake up in bed, the call just a dream.

No such luck. Logan Gabriel won. He had been chosen *Elan Magazine*'s Most Eligible Bachelor of the Year. A camera crew was on its way right now to A mbient Marketing, where he worked, to break the news and whisk him away for a six-week adventure as a result of the contest.

Only he had no idea he'd even entered it.

What had she done? Her plan to get Logan to notice her just sprouted legs and was running right at her. This must have been how Logan felt when she tackled him in the championship game when they were kids. No wonder she had been permanently reduced to friend status.

A stab of pain hit her between the eyes, and she pressed the heel of her hand against it. She wanted Logan to think of her differently, to see her as more than his friend. She looked at her watch. In about thirty minutes, she would get her wish. And not in a good way.

She grabbed her purse and keys and practically dove into the front seat of her car. As she backed out of her driveway, she activated the Bluetooth and called the one person she could count on to help her break the news to Logan, if only they could get to Ambient before the camera crew came.

"Patt, I'm a dead woman if you can't get to Logan in the next twenty minutes and get him out of his office," she screamed when the call connected.

"Slow down, girl," Patt said from the other end of the line. "That all sounded like one big word. Calm down, and tell me what you need."

Rikka inhaled and blew out a long breath of air to try to calm her nerves. "You have to meet me at Logan's office right now."

"Why?"

"Remember the picture I sent to *Elan*?"

"Uh-huh, do I ever. The man looked hotter than the Sahara Desert."

"Too hot apparently, because I won. I mean, he won." Silence preceded an uproar of laughter on the other end of the line, making Rikka turn down the volume on the car radio through which the call played. "Stop laughing, and help me," she pleaded.

The laughter weakened to snickers. "You know I will. I just can't help imaging the look on Logan's face when the next issue comes out. The picture you sent in made him look like he didn't have anything on but a big ole fern leaf."

"Camera angle," Rikka said through clenched teeth. "You know very well he had on a bathing suit."

"I know that, and you know that. But when that picture winds up in the center of the magazine, millions of ladies won't care when they're staring at the staple in his navel."

Rikka groaned. "The picture is the least of my problems. I didn't read the small print on the entry form." She slowed the car to a stop as the light ahead turned red.

"And it said?"

"He's about to be taken right from work to an estate in Morris County."

"That doesn't sound so bad."

"It's worse than bad. The contest was actually a photo audition for a reality TV show. There are six women also going to the estate. One gets kicked out once a week until he finds Ms. Right for a ten-day dream vacation to Maui."

"You entered him in a reality TV show?" Patt spaced the words evenly, as though contemplating each one.

"It appears so."

"Oooh, bummer for you. Logan's been your dream date since grade school, and now you have some handpicked competition."

"My dream date is turning into a Stephen King nightmare."

"Girl, I told you not to do this. A six-foot, dark-haired, blue-eyed, body-like-a-god hunk alone for six weeks with six women, huh? A lot can happen in a month and a half."

"Not if I can help it because, actually, I'm going, too."

"You're one of the six women?"

Rikka heaved a sigh. "No, I'm the one who has to help him pick one of the six women."

"Shut—*up*." Patt's tone was full of disbelief.

"Shutting up won't solve the problem."

Patt snickered. "Maybe you shouldn't have signed his name on the entry form."

Rikka eased her car onto the interstate. "Maybe I shouldn't have signed mine."

Logan Gabriel ditched his suit jacket and rolled up the sleeves of his white cotton shirt to his elbows. He still had a lot of work to do on the PowerPoint presentation for the three o'clock meeting with the new client. Hopefully, the marketing campaign would mean a multimillion-dollar contract for the ad agency and a hefty commission for him. He did have his eye on a new Beamer. Convertible. 325i. One sweet ride.

Since he'd gotten his master's degree in marketing after a stint at a party college in New Hampshire, he'd settled in and been steadily climbing the corporate ladder. Despite his father's insistence he make it a priority to excel in football in college, he'd been only marginally interested in sports since discovering business tactics as a freshman. Now at thirty, he worked hard and could be named a junior partner in the firm.

And he could all but cement that promotion by landing the Bio-Shoes account.

The door to his office opened, and Bob Kiernan, a sixty-something full partner with a shrewd but creative mind, stepped in. "How's the footwear ad coming?"

Logan swung the laptop he'd been working on toward Kiernan and started the presentation. "Take a look."

Kiernan watched for a while. "Impressive."

Logan paused the slideshow. "I have a few more adjustments to make, but I think I can sell it."

"You know Sherwin's retiring," Kiernan said, turning and walking toward the door. "Junior partner pays twenty-five percent more with an annual bonus, based on productivity, and an assistant to help with the paperwork." He pointed to the laptop. "Provided you close the deal."

Logan immediately calculated the difference in salary and thought of three or four investment possibilities. "I'll close the deal all right. You just make sure the corner office is repainted in time for me to move in on Monday."

"There's another project you'll have to deal with first," Kiernan said. "But it's more of a fun thing than a work thing. We're very excited about it."

Logan felt his brow furrow. "And what one would that be?"

Kiernan patted Logan on the shoulder. "Want it to be a surprise for the partners, do you?" He made a zipping motion across his mouth. "Mum's the word." Then he saluted Logan and closed the office door on his way out.

Logan stared at the door for a while. What the heck was Kiernan talking about? The man was always cryptic and loved throwing coworkers offtrack. Logan looked at the laptop screen as the slide show finished. No sense trying to figure it out now. He had a multimillion-dollar pitch to make.

He ran the presentation again, his future entirely in his own hands and the memory stick of his flash drive. The sale was in the details, so he pressed the enter key and watched the ad campaign run another time, just to be sure his proverbial ducks were all in a row.

He watched the blonde model he'd hired run across the set in the Arizona desert with her beautiful feet in white running shoes. As he contemplated the ad sale, a clammy feeling suddenly started in his stomach. He recognized it as the same clammy feeling he got just before something happened to change the course he had set for himself. It was the same feeling he got right before he decided not to run with the bulls in Pamplona when his friend did and got gored, the same feeling that kept him from skydiving, the same feeling that seemed to warn him about needy women.

And it was the same feeling he remembered having when he was in Pee Wee football, right before he got tackled by Rikka McAllister in the championship game.

He tossed his shoulders. Wow. Weird. Though he saw Rikka all the time, he hadn't thought about that particular game in a while. He shook the thought from his mind and pushed the call button for the receptionist.

"Yes, Mr. Gabriel?" she replied.

"Angie, I'll need you to hold all calls for the next few hours. No one disturbs me."

He barely had the last word out of his mouth when he heard a commotion outside his door. He looked up in time to see Rikka burst through it, Angie right on her heels.

"We have to leave right now!" Rikka shouted at him.

Angie put herself between Rikka and Logan. "I'm sorry, Mr. Gabriel. I tried to stop her, but she pushed right by me." She put her hand on Rikka's arm. "You'll have to leave now. Mr. Gabriel is busy."

Rikka shrugged it away. "Doesn't look that way." She walked around the desk, grabbed the briefcase she saw on the floor, and began throwing papers into it. Then she pulled back Logan's chair. "We really need to leave."

He turned to her, and Rikka suddenly felt as though she couldn't breathe. Haloed in light from the window behind him, Logan looked almost angelic. His square chin seemed sculpted, his cheekbones defined like a decisive stroke of an artist's brush. She fought to keep her face neutral. He came across as so appealing, even though the look in his ice-blue eyes was one of the most confused expressions she had ever seen on a person's face.

Logan took the briefcase from her hands, shut it, and put it back on the floor. "Freddy, what are you doing here?"

"I wish you'd stop calling me that."

"Sorry. Habit."

She grabbed his arm. "We can work on that later. We really have to go."

Angie shouldered past her. "Should I call security, Mr. Gabriel?"

"No, Angie, Freddy is…"

"Rikka," she corrected.

His eyes narrowed thoughtfully. "Rikka and I are friends." Angie looked back and forth between them a few times. "Really. It's okay," he assured. "You can go, Angie."

Angie gave them each one more glance, then nodded and left.

"Now," Logan said, turning to Rikka. "Want to tell me what's going on, Freddy?"

"I don't want you to call me that anymore."

Logan grinned. "You came all the way to Morristown to tell me that?"

His playful smile tripped her heartstrings. She hoped it wasn't the last one she would see, especially when he found out what she had done. She put her hands together like she was praying. "No, but I really need to talk to you, and I need to do it now."

He gestured to the chair opposite his desk. "So talk."

"Not here."

"Why?"

"Because."

"We're not in school, so that's not going to work."

Rikka checked her watch. She was running out of time. She figured she had about two minutes to get Logan out the back door before the camera crew came in the front.

She put both hands on his shoulders. "Do you trust me?"

His brow furrowed. "Do I have reason not to?"

She pushed his chair back and began to drag him to his feet. "No. Yes. Maybe."

"Which one is it?" he asked, standing.

Almost at the same time, his office door opened. Rikka felt her heart drop to her knees. Fear stopped her from turning around.

But Patt's distinctive voice gave her renewed hope. "You, you beat me here." She closed the door behind her. "What's the plan?"

"Thank heavens it's only you." Rikka latched onto Logan's right arm with the intensity of a death grip and gestured to his left with a lift of her chin. "Help me get him out of here."

Patt grabbed on and together they started to drag him to the door.

Logan tried to dig his heels into the thick carpeting. "Stop."

"No time," Rikka said, still trying to get him out the door.

Logan grabbed onto the door frame with both hands. "I have a bad feeling about this. Tell me what's going on."

Rikka tried to pry his fingers free. "Nonsense. Everything's fine."

"I sincerely doubt it," he replied in protest, just as she and Patt manhandled him out the door. Angie appeared frozen in place as she watched them from her desk chair in silence, telephone receiver pressed against her ear.

The trio had just gotten into the hallway when they were blinded by bright lights. A microphone boom appeared over their heads while a cameraman leaned in to get the shot with his remote.

"Congratulations, Logan Gabriel," a clearly feminine voice said, a national TV station logo recognizable on the microphone in her hand. "You have been chosen as *Elan Magazine*'s Most Eligible Bachelor. Tell the country how you feel." She held out the microphone to him and waited for his response.

Rikka looked at a monitor being held to her left. Captured on it, probably for later viewing as an intro to the show, she and Patt looked like deer caught in headlights, holding on to the arms of the man who was already on the cover of the magazine the reporter held in her hand.

"What?" Logan asked.

"You've won."

"Won what?"

"The title of *Elan Magazine*'s Most Eligible Bachelor and the chance to meet six bachelorettes, one of whom you will choose for an adventure of a lifetime."

The reporter held up the magazine. Logan took it with both hands. Not only was he on the cover, but he recognized it as a picture taken at the backyard pool of his mother's house. The strategic placing of some branches through which the shot had been snapped made it seem as though he'd been posing naked for it.

His eyes widened. There could be only one angle from which the shot had been taken. From the neighbors' backyard. The McAllisters'.

He turned, magazine in hand. "Freddy!"

"Rikka," she said in a small voice as Patt laughed and pulled out her cell phone to take pictures. She looked from the picture to Logan's face. "My bad."

Mr. Kiernan appeared in the hallway and pushed his way through the camera techies. "You are a genius, Gabriel."

"I am?"

"Certainly. This is a great opportunity for the firm. You'll be on national television, and so will we, by association. Great exposure." Kiernan patted Logan's shoulder. "Terrific exposure."

Patt looked at the magazine cover. "I'll say."

Rikka swiveled her head and gave Patt the keep-quiet look.

"And you are?" the woman with the mike in her hand asked, angling it toward Kiernan.

"I'm the bachelor's boss." He sounded like a proud father.

"Tell me how you feel about this," she pressed.

Rikka could hear a few of his words as the TV crew turned the cameras on Kiernan. "Clients. Partners. Business." She didn't have to hear more to know Logan's boss was on board with the idea. Maybe it would be all right after all. If his boss wanted Logan to do this, maybe Logan would.

A crew member pulled Logan inside the ring of reporters and placed him next to Kiernan, who looped an arm across his shoulders. "Yes, this is one of our brightest stars," Kiernan said. "And I'll just bet he's going to be one of prime time's, too."

The itchy feeling Rikka had earlier crawled its way up her spine in concert with the annoyed look spreading across Logan's face.

"What about my clients, Mr. Kiernan?" Logan asked, blinking against the bright light.

"They'll be temporarily reassigned. Don't worry about anything except having a good time and getting the right amount of publicity for the firm." Then he hugged Logan like he would a six-year-old. "Pull this off and the junior partnership is a slam dunk."

The attention then shifted to Rikka. Someone pushed her next to Logan.

The reporter thrust the microphone in her face. "Tell America why you entered Mr. Gabriel in the contest, Ms. McAllister."

Logan crossed his arms over his chest. "Yes, do tell America," he agreed.

Rikka looked from Logan to the reporter to Patt and then around the crowded hallway. It seemed like every employee in the building had come out of their offices and was waiting for her answer.

What on earth was she supposed to do now? She couldn't possibly tell them the truth. She couldn't tell anyone. Not now. Maybe not ever.

Chapter Two

Logan and Rikka sat on opposite sides of the bench seat in the back of the stretch limo, so far apart you could have fit two other people between them. Rikka looked out the left side window, Logan, the right. The magazine lay on the seat between them.

Rikka glanced at it several times, more than tempted to slowly walk her fingers over to it and slide it toward her with the intent of tossing it out the window. Not that it would have mattered. In a day or so, every newsstand would have a copy of it.

She looked at Logan, his profile perfectly outlined against the glass. His neutral expression did nothing to take away from the finely sculpted details she loved so much: his nose with the little dent put there from one too many tackles on the football field, his cheekbones shadowed by long lashes.

Her heart hitched. Why *did* she do this? She used phrases like "on a whim" and "never thought we'd win" to successfully answer the reporter's questions. The careful and neutral sound bites bought her some time, but Logan wouldn't be satisfied with anything less than the truth.

But the truth was the one thing she could never bring herself to tell him, almost from the first day they met.

At twelve, her family moved in next door to his, and she thought he was the cutest boy she had ever seen. At fourteen, she couldn't make it through the day if she didn't somehow find a way to talk to him, even though he went to private school and she went to public school. At sixteen, she thought she'd die when he broke her heart without even knowing it by asking Rita Rose Donald to his junior prom. At eighteen, she pretended to be excited when he accepted a college scholarship to New Hampshire State in Henniker, knowing she would be attending community college in the next town.

During their college years, she kept tabs on him through stories his mother shared with her mother or through chats on the Internet. During holidays, when he came home from school, and over summer break, she made sure she saw him at least once a day. When he moved back home after he got his master's degree, she was in heaven. But when he found his own place in another town a year later, she couldn't eat for days.

Her silly schoolgirl crush had taken root in eighth grade and became a living, breathing part of her as the years passed. Sure, she dated, and so did he, but never each other.

Over those same years, when she did try so many ways to get him to notice her as more than just a friend, all she managed to get from him were comments like "Skirt's too short, Fred" or "The smoky eye thing is not working for you. You look like a raccoon."

To him, she was Freddy McAllister, right tackle and the "little sister" he never had.

The only thing she did have on her side was the unwritten rule that neither of them could bring anyone else to the get-togethers at The Huddle, a local sports bar, where they met bimonthly with a group of mutual friends. There she had him all to herself, factoring out the other twelve or fifteen people who joined them regularly, of course.

But now she had him for the next month and a half. Sort of, anyway. There was the matter of the six probably gorgeous, model-thin bachelorettes the producers of the TV show had picked out for him. And she did have to hand him over to one of them at the end of the show.

So why *did* she enter his picture in the stupid contest?

Because she had sensed him changing over the last couple of months. He missed more happy hours at The Huddle, seemed more focused on his job, and started talking about buying a home to put down some permanent roots. To her, he sounded like a man getting ready to settle down. She decided that if Logan was about to survey the playing field and find someone to share his future, she needed to make sure she would be in the game.

If somehow, she didn't pick out his soul mate in the process.

After about ten minutes of a silence she had only experienced once before when she had tried a trendy sensory deprivation tank as a lark, she took a deep breath and spoke. "You mad?"

Logan slowly swiveled his head toward her and raised a brow as dark as his hair. He grabbed the magazine and held the cover toward her, saying nothing. Then his eyebrows drew down, as did the corners of his mouth. He looked at her in a kind of wordless challenge filled with a thousand questions.

"You have to admit, it is a nice shot," she said, trying out her best smile.

"I look naked," he countered.

While he didn't return her smile with one of his own, she actually relaxed with the sound of his voice. He didn't seem nearly as mad as he had at the office. For a while, she had thought she might be in for six weeks of silence. Logan could be pretty stubborn.

She took the magazine from him, angling it toward her eyes. "You don't look that naked," she said with a dismissing snicker.

But he did. She'd set the shot up through the bushes on purpose. She actually had to crawl underneath two thick evergreens and between some climbing rosebushes to have some low tree branches at just the right angle to obscure his bathing suit from a point just below his navel. His six-pack abs and toned upper body did the rest.

"I can clearly tell you're getting ready to take a swim," she assured him.

"And where exactly does my bathing suit tell you that?"

She turned the magazine to him and pointed to the lower left corner. "Right here?"

"No, that looks like part of the climbing roses in your mother's yard to me."

"It does?" She flipped the magazine back toward her. "Well then, here." She pointed again.

"Rhododendron."

"Here?"

"Potted geranium."

Rikka sighed and fell back onto the seat. "Okay, okay. I admit it. I took the picture like that on purpose."

"Why?"

Logan could not have imagined the impact that one simple word had on her.

Why? Because he was a man, and she was a woman who appreciated it.

Why? Because she had had a crush on him since they were kids, and he never saw her as anything more than the girl who was cursed to be like a sister to him.

Why? Because she watched him take other girls to the prom, other girls to movies they had talked about seeing, and other girls to dinner and plays and concerts, all the time wishing he had taken her instead.

Why? Because she had it all planned. Enter his picture in the contest and wait for the so-sorry letter. Then show it to him and wait for him to feel flattered when she told him he should have won. Mission accomplished and regrets letter in hand, he would surely notice that she had been noticing him.

"I did it because I think you deserved to win," was all she finally said. "You work long hours. You're a bachelor, and you're eligible. I thought you could use a break and take some time to enjoy an adventure." The lie felt like a knife in her heart.

But for the first time since the camera crew came onto the scene, she thought she saw Logan actually relax. "Thanks, I guess. But can you please explain exactly what you have gotten me into?"

She grimaced. "I thought it was just a little photo contest, but as it turns out, there's more to it."

"Apparently," he agreed. "We're on our way to some mansion for six weeks."

"Did anyone mention to you that in six weeks and one day you're going on a ten-day cruise with the girl of your dreams?" She actually flinched when she said it.

"I believe someone did." Disbelief set in the square of his jaw and echoed in his words.

"I gather that part doesn't make you very happy."

"I have a sales pitch for a million-dollar account scheduled for"—he angled his watch toward his eyes—"an hour ago."

"Your boss said your clients would be temporarily reassigned, remember?"

"There is no 'temporarily' in advertising and marketing, Fred. I could lose all my regulars in six weeks."

She wished he wouldn't call her by her old nickname. It added to the brotherly tone of their relationship. But old habits were hard to break, and she had been Freddy to him since she was twelve.

"I'm sure your clients will wait for you," she assured. "It's probably in the rules somewhere neither of us can lose our jobs because of this."

Logan cut his gaze to her. "What else is in the rules?"

She blew out a long breath of air and waited until he finished brushing back the hair from his forehead. Any other time, the simple gesture would have made him seem casual, relaxed. But couple it with the fire she could see in his eyes that turned them to the color of good sapphires, and it seemed like he might be getting ready for a street fight.

"Actually," she said with a grin she hoped made her look adorable, "I didn't exactly read the rules." The look on his face told her she hadn't produced the desired effect.

"You didn't read the rules." He punctuated each word with a deliberate hesitation.

She threw up her hands in a friendly gesture of resignation, her laugh betraying the nerves she tried to control. "You'd think one would read the rules and especially the fine print before signing the entry form."

"You'd think," he agreed.

"The spokesman did tell me where we'd be going."

When their gazes locked, the frustration in Logan's body kicked up a notch. "And where might that be?"

"You are going to be so excited."

"I can hardly wait."

"We're going to the Villa Soprano in Montville. Maybe you saw it on TV when it was featured on an episode of the *Sopranos* in 2006."

Logan burst out laughing. "Yeah. Sure," he said once he stopped. "But really. Where are we going?"

"No, honest. We're going there. It's been written up in lots of articles about the area, and it's not far from home."

"Wonderful."

The tone of his voice settled on annoyed. She laughed, but more from another bout of nerves than anything else. She gave up with a shrug. "Try to go with it. We're going to be on TV. It'll be fun."

Logan cut his eyes to her. "We'll see."

Chapter Three

The car wound its way across the northern New Jersey countryside. The landscape changed from small towns to houses on acre-sized lots to rural countryside before it made a right onto a private road.

Rikka watched the meticulously manicured grounds pass by out the side window, trying to figure out how to make the best of things and marveling at the landscape. Ten feet back on either side of the road, the grounds were exquisitely kept. Beyond, the vista rolled perfectly into whatever natural ground it bordered, whether field or forest.

Admiring the view, she almost missed it when the limo driver passed through a set of decorative gates that opened to yet another winding road. The car passed a tennis court with a viewing gazebo and a small playhouse until it broke through the tree line and onto a paved driveway arching gently to the left, leading to the magnificent place she would be calling home for a time.

Though she never did see that particular episode, Villa Soprano certainly would have been a fitting home for Tony and the gang. Designed to offer privacy and security, the estate also offered opulence. A turret centered the building, with massive two-story wings extending from each side. The exquisite stone exterior reminded her of a Scottish castle.

A covered porch traced by three graceful arches brought her eye to the beautiful wood and wrought iron entry door. It looked to her like the ultimate dream house for a modern-day princess.

She waited until the limo driver rounded the car and opened the car door for her. Logan hadn't waited. He stood beside the driver.

"Some house, huh?" she said to him.

"Impressive, to say the least."

They walked toward the front door, and it burst open. An impeccably dressed man, hair more sculpted than styled, carrying a clipboard in one hand, spread his arms wide in greeting.

"Hello. Hello. Welcome to the Villa Soprano and *Eligible Bachelor*." He sprang down the front steps. Behind him, a smartly dressed woman waited in the doorway. "I'm Roberto, one of the producers." He pointed behind him. "And that's Annie, my assistant. You'll be seeing a lot of her. She'll be more involved with the day-to-day necessities." He held up the clipboard and shuffled through the papers attached. He pointed to Logan. "So you're our bachelor."

Logan extended his hand. "Apparently so."

Roberto ignored the offer of a handshake and flipped the papers on the clipboard. He looked up, a note of disapproval on his face. "And you're Frederika." He tsk-tsked. "That name will never do. Too dated. We'll rename you for the show."

"How about calling her Freddy," Logan offered, apparently seizing the opportunity for a little payback.

"No!" Rikka shouted.

"Yes!" Roberto agreed.

"No!" Rikka emphasized.

"But yes. That will definitely delineate between her and the contenders." Roberto tucked the clipboard under his arm and clapped his hands together in approval. "Freddy it is."

"You can't change my name," she protested.

"Oh, but I can," Roberto returned. He retrieved the clipboard and found the page he wanted. "It says so right here in the contract. The producer," he paused for emphasis, making sure he made eye contact with Rikka, "has the right to temporarily adjust any and all personal matters to make the show more attractive to the audience and prospective sponsors."

"How does my name factor into attracting sponsors?" she asked, hand on hips.

Roberto angled the last paper on the clipboard toward her. "Is that your signature?" he asked, pointing.

"Yes."

"Then that's how it factors in," Roberto said before turning and walking back up the stairs.

Rikka, now back to Freddy for six weeks at least, cast a quick glance at Logan. He was becoming more and more unsuccessful at suppressing the satisfied grin now residing where a frown had been on his face.

Logan caught her looking at him. His smile broke wide. "After you, Freddy," he said with a flourish, stepping back.

Her shoulders slumped as she started up the three steps. "Do you know how long it took me to get rid of that nickname?"

"Nope," Logan returned. "But in a few days that's what millions of reality show junkies will be calling you for the rest of your life."

Freddy glared at him. She guessed she deserved it. Then she pulled her brain out of its death spiral and followed Roberto through the front door. She may as well find out what else he had in store for her.

Her shoes tapped on the gray travertine floor tiles. Her head was on a swivel as she took in the elegant architecture and whiter-than-white walls of the entrance foyer. Enhanced with columns, it defined the entrance and separated it from the great room beyond.

I don't belong here, she thought.

Roberto shifted his clipboard and led them past the great room into the library. The room smelled of rich wood and lemon furniture polish, the ambience warmed by a fire in the stone fireplace that took up an entire wall.

"Sit, sit," he said, taking his place behind a huge cherrywood desk. "We have a lot to cover in a short amount of time."

Freddy plunked herself down on a dark maroon leather chair opposite him. "This place is amazing."

"Yes, it is." Roberto propped his elbow on the desktop. "Three floors are all built around center circles. The lower level has a media room, a wine cellar—of course." He rolled his eyes and continued, "A rec room, exercise room, and access to a six-car garage."

"I think I could live very comfortably down there alone," Freddy cut in.

Roberto shot her a glance, giving her the odd feeling he could see every place she'd been since birth, none of them matching the elegance of the basement of Villa Soprano. She nodded her apology for interrupting him.

He continued. "This main level has six bedrooms with en suite baths to the right of the entrance and everything else to the left, including another media room and a conservatory."

Freddy shifted on the leather chair, her movements making a squishing sound. "What is a conservatory anyway?"

"You like plants?" Logan asked with a lopsided grin.

"Yes."

"Then you'll like the conservatory."

"Oh," Freddy said, drawing out the word. "A greenhouse." She turned back to Roberto. "Why didn't you just say that?"

He rolled his eyes and went on. "Upstairs to the left is the three-room master suite with master bath spa. That's where you'll be, Logan."

"Am I somewhere downstairs?" Freddy asked.

"No. The circular staircase leading upstairs ends in an open-style balcony connecting the master suite to another bedroom with its own master bath spa, study, and hobby room. Beyond are rooms only used for storage." Roberto pointed at Freddy. "That's your side."

She blinked in awe of the sheer scope of the estate. "I can't imagine planning something this grand."

"It took about four years. The architect wanted this house to employ ancient geometrical principles including the Fibonacci series and the Golden section, which is apparent in portions of the elevations and floor plan. The architect used all manner of Euclidean geometry tying together the square, rectangle, octagon, hexagon, and circle into this—a pleasing three-dimensional design tapestry."

Freddy shook her head. "What did you just say?" She turned to Logan. "Did you understand any of what he just said?"

Logan tented his fingers and rested his forefingers on his lips to cover the smirk.

"Of course you did. You're in marketing. You have to know everything."

Roberto sighed. "But the only thing you have to know is that the top level is off limits to the film crew. Everywhere else, there will be either people following you with handheld cameras or remotes that can track everything. Plus, whenever you are on the lower levels, you need to be miked, so Annie," he said, gesturing to her sitting quietly in a chair at the back of the room, "will show you how to use the mikes along with anything else we need to do to make the show a success. She'll also be the go-to person if either of you need anything."

Freddy raised her hand. "I need everything. Pj's, makeup, shoes, clothes."

Roberto pulled two sheets of paper from the clipboard and handed one to Freddy and one to Logan. "You're a little ahead of me. When you get upstairs, you'll both find closets packed with most of what you'll need during your stay here. Anything else you want, fill out this form and Annie will arrange to get it for you."

Freddy raised her hand again. "How do you know what size I am?"

Roberto sighed as if in annoyance. "Average dress size. Shoes, seven. Bra size…"

This time Freddy's hand shot out in warning. "Don't go there." She glanced at Logan. He appeared to be paying a lot more attention to Roberto. She hitched her thumb toward him. "What about our bachelor here?"

Roberto didn't miss a beat. "Forty regular, with a thirty-two-inch waist, a departure from the six-inch norm." He leaned forward and assessed Logan. "You work out, right?"

Logan nodded.

"Shoe size, ten. Briefs, thirty-two."

Freddy's mouth dropped open as her mind used what Roberto described to put together a perfect picture of Logan standing in the entrance foyer with a dozen roses in his hand. "Boxers or tighty whities?" she whispered almost breathlessly.

Logan leaned over to her, his hand still covering his mouth. "Freddy, what are you doing?"

"Research," she whispered back. "Shh. Let the man continue."

Roberto pursed his lips and not in amusement. "Depends on what he's wearing. Can't have the package outlined on prime time TV when the kiddies might be watching."

Freddy felt her cheeks warm from what had to be a blush when she saw Logan's grin break wide.

Roberto rescued her from the awkward moment. "Can we go on please? We have a lot of detail to cover and not much time to do it. The women will be coming in tomorrow evening for a short reception before starting the competition. Logan will wear a tuxedo when he greets them." He pointed at Freddy. "And I suggest that you go through your closet and pick out something suitable. We have a whole wardrobe department on standby if you can't find something you like or that fits properly."

"I thought you said you knew my size," Freddy countered.

"You do know the average American woman is a size fourteen, and the average reality show woman is a size two." He looked her over, from shoes to hairline. "We may need to do some alterations with you."

"Are you saying I'm fat?" Freddy asked him, punctuating the last word between clenched teeth. She felt her nostrils flair.

Logan's hand on her arm was the only thing that prevented her from jumping over the desk. "He means you have curves, and they don't. Isn't that right, Roberto?"

Roberto leaned back and clasped his hands over his chest. "Mostly."

"I can't do this," Freddy said after a few moments of silence. "There has to be a way out." An edgy feeling she couldn't control built inside her. "Maybe some creative accounting so the network doesn't lose money if the show doesn't air?"

"Creative accountants and people who try to break contracts often end up in court," Roberto offered.

Freddy looked at him. Roberto's face read dead serious. He flipped through the papers on the clipboard and detached a stack before sliding them across the desktop to her.

"I'll leave you a copy of the entry contract you signed and give you time to review it overnight. I think you'll find everything has been spelled out quite clearly. We can meet again tomorrow after breakfast to go over anything you might not understand or want to understand."

She frowned at his dry tone. "I don't like your attitude. Maybe the network can send someone else."

"Good luck with that request." Roberto's voice projected confidence.

"I'd need luck?"

"Because I asked Uncle Efron for this show, and nothing is going to stop it from airing. It's going to earn me an Emmy."

"Uncle Efron?"

"Efron Canterwilde III, the executive producer. My mother's brother."

"Oh, great," Freddy said, sinking back down into the leather chair.

Roberto smiled with the victory. "Now, let's go over some of the basics of what we expect of both of you, shall we?"

Logan and Freddy looked at each other. What other option did they really have?

Chapter Four

Freddy roamed the top floor of the mansion. She could hear noise coming from Logan's side. Sometimes it sounded like doors banging, and sometimes it sounded like water running. She couldn't imagine what was going on.

Maybe she should go over there and offer to help him settle in. She started to walk across the connecting walkway and stopped. Considering the situation in which she'd put him, maybe she should just mind her own business for once. She walked back toward her own suite. At least two more times, her mind flipped one way and then the other until she felt like a sentinel walking a war post.

This was ridiculous. She took a deep breath. She was going over there. At his doorway, she pasted on what she hoped was a charming smile and lifted her hand to knock. But as the thought of sharing the upper level of the mansion with him for the next six weeks flashed across her mind, her fist stopped an inch before it struck the door as she suffered what she was sure was a hot flash. She really wanted to share something significant with Logan; something more than "Pass the fries" at a fast-food place. Had wanted to since she began to think of him as more than just a running back on the opposing football team when she was a kid. She just never thought it would be sharing a house with him with the goal of getting him a date with someone else.

Too far past the time to worry about that now, she blew out a long breath of air and finally knocked. "Logan," she called out, "I heard you slamming doors and hoped it wasn't on my account."

"It is, but come in anyway," she heard him call back.

She couldn't see him when she first stepped into the room. "Logan?"

"In here."

He stepped out from inside the room beyond a second doorway, boyish wonder in his eyes as he leaned on the door frame. When he looked at her, she found herself so captivated by his eyes that she barely heard him speak.

"You have got to see this."

She raised her face to the ceiling to gather herself after he disappeared back inside. In this intimate setting, she felt a little weak in the knees. The thought of walking around his bedroom generated enough heat inside her to make her feel like she was walking into a furnace.

"Come in here," he said, reappearing briefly.

She took a deep breath and followed him into a room larger than the whole downstairs of her house. Built-in shelves covered with shoes, accessories, and neatly folded shirts lined the wall to the right. To the left, a thickly upholstered loveseat and matching chair with a small table between them sat in front of two sets of French doors. A mirror covered part of the wall behind her and the door on the opposite side led to the master spa.

"Over here." Logan gestured for Freddy to sit on one of the chairs and opened one of the sets of closet doors. Inside, two rows of bars filled with shirts and trousers were divided by rows of drawers.

"And look at this," he said, walking to the center island and pulling open the drawers.

Freddy swallowed hard, praying he didn't notice. She hoped she wasn't about to look at his underwear. Oh well, she decided, at least she'd get the answer to her earlier question: boxers or briefs? At this point, who cared? He probably looked great in either one. She peeked over. The drawers were packed with stuff.

"Socks, jeans, gym pants." He walked back to the closet. "Suits, dress shirts, polos, khakis." He stepped back and turned in a small circle. "Can you believe this stuff? The list I gave the assistant earlier had two entries—my favorite blue jeans and my robe. I may never wear them."

Lordy, she thought, *don't say that.* She pictured him naked and made a mental note to poke out her mind's eye.

He swiveled his head and shot her one of the devastating grins she'd come to know over the years. Now all she wanted to do was grab his cheeks and kiss him the way she always had in her dreams. The urge to find out if reality could be as perfect as fantasy grew inside her as fast as weeds did on a New Jersey lawn on a hot summer day. With each second passing, every feminine hormone in her body shouted, *Kiss him, stupid,* until all their tempting voices blurred into one big buzz inside her head.

She stood up and put as much distance between them as the room allowed, trying not to act on the building urge. "How can you possibly wear all this stuff in six weeks?" she asked him, lightly fingering the shirts neatly folded on the shelves on the opposite wall.

He shrugged. "Don't know, but everything seems to be my size. That alone amazes me."

"I did have to put down a physical description on the entry form."

His hand was on a pair of jeans. "Exactly what did you describe?"

"The form asked for height, weight, build, stuff like that." She left out the part about the narrative she'd added, suddenly embarrassed by the detail she had gone into about his likes and dislikes. From the look of everything in the walk-in closet, someone had taken her word as gospel.

"Do you have the same thing in your room?" he asked her.

She felt her cheeks warm in a blush. "To be honest, I spent most of the last few hours sitting on a chair in a daze and didn't get past the bedroom. I was trying to wrap my head around what happened when I heard doors slam and thought you might be trying to escape."

Logan laughed. "Back at the office, I thought seriously about skipping out on the whole idea, but when I saw how much my boss was into this, and what it could mean to my career, I figured I'd ride it out and see what happened."

Freddy felt her stomach clench. He actually sounded happy. She wasn't sure if that could be a good thing or a bad thing, considering he was about to spend the next six weeks getting to know women better, none of them her.

"So you're not mad anymore then?" she asked tentatively.

"More overwhelmed than anything."

"Me, too," she admitted. "Starting tomorrow, there are going to be a lot of people around here poking microphones and lights in our faces." An odd mixture of fear and disappointment suddenly rifled through her as she realized the next few hours might be the only ones they would have together without the entire country watching them on TV. She began to pace. "We're going to be miked and followed and then edited. Who knows what's going to be aired." She stopped and put a hand to her stomach. "I think I'm going to be sick." Most of the blood left her head, and the room began to spin.

Logan reacted instantly. He grabbed her shoulders and dragged her back to the chaise. "Don't move. I'm going to get you some water."

She leaned her head back onto the padded backrest and closed her eyes to stop the spinning. What had she done? The enormity of how unprepared she was for this hit her hard.

"Fred. Are you all right?"

His voice sounded like an echo. She wanted to respond, but she couldn't find the energy. She heard him slide something onto a tabletop next to the chaise. Still, she couldn't open her eyes.

"Fred. Answer me." He patted her hand as he spoke.

With great effort, she fluttered her eyes open and was immediately hit by the full force of concern she saw on his face. "I'm okay."

He didn't let go of her hand when he sat on the edge of the chaise. "You scared me. I thought you were going to faint for a moment."

Her heart pounded. She didn't know if it was from fear of the unknown or the fact that he held her hand. "It seemed like a distinct possibility for a while."

He reached over and retrieved the glass of water. "Here."

She cupped the glass with both hands and held on for dear life.

"Look. We don't have to do this," he said. "It's not worth all the stress I see on your face. There must be some way we can get out of the contract."

Just so she could stop looking into his eyes, she glanced at the glass before raising it to her lips. "You're not interested in finding the woman of your dreams?" Her heart beat faster, and she hoped her voice held no more emotion than it would have if she'd asked him if he wanted to watch football or hockey.

"Actually, I have been thinking about that," he admitted.

Freddy felt her heart slam to a stop as though it hit a brick wall.

"Someday. But not quite this way and not in just a few weeks."

Slowly, her heart seemed to restart.

"But then again, you are going to help me, right?"

And stop again.

"So it could be fun."

"Fun," she agreed weakly. Whom was she kidding? There would be no fun. Not for her. It was going to be pure torture.

Besides, Roberto had all but said there could be no turning back now. There had to be some sort of penalty clause in the contract she hadn't bothered to read. In a day or two, the magazine would hit the stands, the manor was rented, the sponsors had paid their bills, and tomorrow, the women would be arriving at the expense of the network. Hundreds of thousands of dollars were at stake here.

She did a quick mental inventory to figure out if she had enough body parts to sell to repay the network if they backed out. Not nearly enough, she decided. She was stuck in a trap of her own making with no way out except straight ahead to the end. She suddenly pictured herself waving good-bye to Logan and the woman she helped pick out for him. It made her feel sick again.

"I think I should go back to my room now."

"Are you sure?"

"Uh-huh. I want to see if I have goodies in my closet, too," she said as an excuse. She gulped down the rest of the water and stood, willing the room to hold still as she made a hasty, but somewhat wobbly exit.

Freddy shut the door to her room and leaned her head against it. Across the connecting walkway, the man of her dreams was preparing to meet six women: all of them on their best behavior, all of them probably model-hot, and all of them ready and willing to walk through fire to get his attention.

And if she had anything to do with it, that's exactly what they'd have to do.

Hand on the brass doorknob to her room, she briefly considered turning the lock. Why bother? Logan wasn't about to invade her personal space anytime soon, except maybe to put a pillow over her face to smother her for what she had done to him.

But it was easy enough for her to imagine something entirely different without even trying. If she had her own reality TV show, his six-foot-two-inches of total charm and sex appeal would appear in the doorway, sweep her off her feet, and go on the date of her dreams. But that had little chance of actually happening. The show was called *Eligible Bachelor*, not *Fantasy Island*.

She took a calming, much-needed breath. Being with Logan in his suite took every bit of self-restraint she had. The time they spent together in his closet had been the closest she'd ever got to kissing him, discounting the quick New Year's Eve peck she got every year at the annual party they attended with friends.

Her impulsiveness and desire to show Logan once and for all she was more than just Freddy McAllister—man's best friend and tackling dummy—had gotten her into this mess. Somehow, she would have to figure out a way to show him the girl of his dreams had always been in front of him.

She shook her head and sat down on the edge of the bed. She had this one night to plan her strategy. One night to somehow embed herself inside his mind so he would compare all the women he was about to meet to her and not want any of them.

She had one night to find out what he really disliked in a woman so she could use it to her advantage somehow.

Suddenly, lightning flashed outside her window. A few seconds later came the distinct rumble of thunder. She walked to the window and looked out. On the grounds below, she could see people scrambling. *Probably camera techies trying to cover outside equipment before it rained*, she thought.

She walked to the desk against the back wall of the room. She still had to fill out the form for what she needed the production assistants to get for her from home. She picked it up and wondered if she could include "a healthy dose of *think first*" on it but opted to walk around and see what had been made available to her instead.

Another large flash of white light suddenly lit the room with a near-simultaneous boom of thunder, shaking the estate almost as soon as she entered the huge walk-in closet. Startled, she stopped in her tracks just as the lights went out and the room turned black.

Chapter Five

The darkness seemed nearly total, even with the small skylight overhead. Heart thudding, and this time not because of Logan but rather from being in the dark in a strange house, Freddy inched her way to the side of the room, listening to the sound of the rain pounding the roof. Everything else seemed quiet and black. She may as well be wearing a blindfold.

Willing her eyes to adjust, her hand found the edge of one of the closets just as she heard the door to her suite open.

"Freddy? You okay?" Logan called to her.

"I'm fine," she called back.

"We lost power."

"Apparently. Maybe one of the camera techs dropped an extension cord in the water or something." She followed the edge of the door to the wall and the wall around to a dresser inside the suite. She inched her way across the dresser top with her hands and hit something smooth and round. The sound of breaking glass followed.

"What happened?" Logan's voice sounded close.

"I think I just destroyed something expensive."

"Don't move, there are probably shards all over the floor."

"What makes you think I'm barefoot?"

She heard his laugh. "Because I am."

Great, she thought. What else didn't he have on? She heard a rustling noise and then a soft thump before something brushed her feet.

"Okay, walk toward the sound of my voice. It's safe now."

Oh no it isn't, she thought, hoping she hadn't said it out loud. "What do you mean?"

"I pulled the blanket off the bed and tossed it on the floor."

"Pretty creative of you." She heard a rumble of thunder, or was it his laugh? For her, both were equally deep and exciting.

"I am in marketing and PR. I have to be creative. Using my imagination is among my best qualities."

"Along with humility," she said with a laugh.

"Yep. Imagination is second, humility is third."

"Then what is…" She stopped. "Never mind. Where are you?" Her hand patted the air in front of her, searching for something solid as she moved toward his voice.

"Right here."

She bumped into him, and he steadied her by slipping his arm around her waist, his hand near her hip. The contact sent a zing of excitement up her spine. Could he see her? Was infrared vision his first best quality? She took in a breath as the heat from his palm snaked up her spine and spread through her body.

Carpe diem, her mind screamed. Seize the day. If she took just one step, she could wrap her arms around him. Another small step and she could touch her lips to his and finally get the kiss she'd imagined about a million times since the eighth grade. Carpe diem. Smart, those ancient Romans and their Latin wisdom. It was now or never.

In anticipation, she tilted her head and started to lean toward him with parted lips when light flashed again. In the finite moment in which they were suspended in the illumination, she could see Logan's gaze lowering to her mouth, which she managed to place only about an inch from his. He looked back into her eyes and his arm tightened around her.

And then the blackness came again.

She expected the explosion of thunder to come, but not the long, slow breath she heard Logan let out as if to steady himself. Quickly, she pulled back. "I guess I misjudged where you were," she said as the thunder silenced.

"Did you?" he whispered.

The warmth coming from his body enveloped her along with his earthy, male scent that mixed perfectly with the smell of summer rain. She inhaled deeply to capture it. "Yes. It's dark in here."

In the ensuing flashes of lightning, she memorized the way he looked in the muted light. The angles of his jaw, the shape of his mouth, the way his hair framed his face—she committed each to memory like frames on film so she could fantasize later, after she explained away the idiotic look she probably had on her face.

"We should light some candles," she muttered, not knowing what else to say.

In the next flash of light, she saw his gaze still on her mouth. Her chest nearly burst as the breath she had trapped there begged for release.

His lips parted. "Lighting candles could be dangerous. Something could catch fire."

Something already had. She already felt that kind of heat from his very warm hand on her back. "Maybe we should get a flashlight," she whispered.

"We could."

She lifted her face toward the sound of his voice, still aching to kiss him. But he released her from his arms. She could feel the warmth fade when he stepped back.

"Wait here. There has to be a flashlight or two in that oversized kitchen."

She could hear him moving toward the door, and her heart sank. She didn't know if she would get another opportunity to be alone with him like this once the other women arrived tomorrow. She hit her forehead with the palm of her hand. She'd make a horrible Roman. Carpe diem. She'd seized nothing. Then she heard him stop at the door.

"You know something, for a minute there, I thought you were going to kiss me," he said.

Freddy panicked. What should she do now?

Carpe diem, her mind shouted again. Heartbeat rising, she started making her way to him, determined another moment would not get away.

"But I'm sure it was just my imagination," he continued. "After all these years, if something was going to happen between us, it probably would have by now."

Freddy nearly broke an ankle stopping in her tracks. She heard him laugh, his footsteps fading as he walked down the hallway. Her heart thudded to a stop. Now she really knew how he felt when the championship had been snatched out of his hands as she tackled him all those years ago.

Logan made his way around the gourmet kitchen, opening and closing drawers with absolutely no idea if a flashlight even existed in the mansion. Offering to get one had only been an excuse. The way Freddy looked when the lightning illuminated the room made him feel as though the bolt hit him squarely in the heart. He needed to get out of the room before he did something stupid. Like kiss her.

He leaned his hip against the granite countertop and let out a long, slow breath, laughing as he did. Imagine that. Him kissing Freddy. She'd probably slap him silly if he tried it.

Another sudden burst of light washed the room making him think about what a previous bolt of lightning revealed to him upstairs:

full lips, closed eyes, all accompanied by a sense of anticipation charging the room. For that one brief moment, it seemed as though Freddy was inviting him to lean forward and make his move.

But that couldn't be right.

Could it?

He never thought about Freddy as anything more than a good friend. But those few, brief seconds he saw her lips open, awash with the stark white light, she looked both innocent and inviting. He could not take his mind off the way he felt at that moment. The basic and very feral male urge to kiss her came upon him as sudden as the lightning that flashed overhead.

He gripped the counter with both hands, hoping to channel the raw energy the memory ignited. Was it simply the circumstances making him think of her more like a very appealing woman rather than his friend for those short, fevered moments? Or could he have feelings for her buried under the years of friendship, coming out only now that their sense of familiarity had been tested under unexpected circumstances?

Still struggling for an answer, he heard the French doors open and turned toward them.

"Mr. Gabriel?"

"Yes." With the dim light outside, Logan could only make out a silhouette.

A beam of light approached and then ran up the cabinets next to him. "Marty from the crew here. I thought you could use a flashlight. I think lightning hit a transformer. The utility company is on its way."

Logan's eyes adjusted to the added light, and he took the flashlight from Marty's outstretched hand. "Is Ms. McAllister okay?" Marty asked.

"She's upstairs. I told her to stay put until I got back."

"The power should be back on within the hour."

"Great. I'll tell her."

"Maybe you two should stay together until then," Marty suggested as he went back outside.

"Will do." Logan replied, happy Marty could not possibly see the big smile the suggestion had brought to his face.

Logan aimed the light ahead of him and walked to the staircase, suddenly hoping the power company was overloaded with outages. Shining the beam on the stairs, he took them two at a time. Another bolt of lightning hit just as he reached the top. The urge to see Freddy bathed in white light again made him almost race toward her suite.

"Logan, is that you?" he heard her call out when the beam from the flashlight hit the threshold of her door.

"Yep, unless you'd rather it be one of the crew."

"I've seen the crew. You're cuter." Her voice sounded playful to him.

"Really now?"

"Don't let it go to your head. I didn't say how much cuter." She stepped closer to the circle of light. "Was there only one flashlight?"

"Marty from the production crew gave it to me." He felt disappointment well up inside him with the idea that she only wanted a flashlight from him. He shook the uncharacteristic feeling away with a toss of his shoulders. "He said lightning hit a transformer, and the power company was on the way to fix it."

"I really don't want to stand here in the dark and wait for them. Do you think there are some candles downstairs we could use?"

He inched the light up, making sure he didn't shine it in her eyes. "Probably enough in the dining room alone to light the house. But we could get light back any minute if we're lucky." *And if we're really lucky, not at all tonight,* he silently added.

"Mentioning the dining room made me realize how hungry I am."

"I would imagine the refrigerator is stocked." He took her hand and pointed the light toward the staircase. "Let's forage. But stay close. Neither of us is familiar with this place, and the stairs in the dark may be tricky."

He kept his eyes on the light guiding them, enjoying the way her small hand fit with his. Slowly, they made their way down the stairs and into the kitchen. Flashes from the lightning helped them find the refrigerator.

"So what do you want?" he asked, moving the light across the shelves.

He felt her lean against his back when her voice came from over his shoulder. "A little of everything. Stress makes me want to eat."

His mind zeroed in on the way her body seemed to melt into his. It felt like spontaneous combustion across his back. He had to get her to move away or risk melting the butter he saw on the refrigerator's second shelf. Resting the flashlight on the counter, he spun around and took her hips with both hands before hoisting her up onto the granite countertop.

"Sit here for a minute. I want to rummage around the kitchen for a minute."

"And I can't help you?"

"I need space."

"By all means then, don't let me stop you." He opened and closed drawers, taking quick inventory while she talked. "Tomorrow's the big day. Your dates are arriving. Are you excited?"

Her voice sounded shaky to him. "I'm more excited about the selection of cheeses I saw in the fridge."

She shifted on the countertop, and the flashlight fell, rolling to the base of the island in the center of the kitchen. The moving light cast eerie shadows across the room, making it appear as though an 8mm film played.

Logan picked the flashlight up once it stopped moving, but it went out. He whacked it against the palm of his hand. It came on with the third hit, centering Freddy in its soft, artificial light. He hadn't intended to put her in the spotlight, but he had to admit, she looked great in it.

"I think the battery may be dying." Not that he cared. The dark could afford him a little more freedom to think about finishing what almost happened upstairs. He raised his eyes and mouthed a prayer of thanks to whatever gods had just smiled on him. The gods of the blind date perhaps. The thought made him chuckle.

"What's so funny?" Freddy asked as his laugh faded. "This all feels pretty creepy to me. Like a scene in one of those Freddy versus Jason movies."

"This mansion is too nice for a horror setting."

"Then the pantry should be stocked with munchies."

He heard her slide off the countertop just as the flashlight flickered again. "Stay put, and let me find the food. You've had the fridge door open too long already, and we don't know how long we'll be without electricity."

"By all means." He handed her the flashlight. "Cook for me."

"Loosely speaking," she agreed, aiming the light inside the open doors of the Sub-Zero refrigerator. "Let's see now. Look. Shrimp cocktail." She hit him in the chest with the light. "Hold this so I can get the tray out."

He stood behind her as she reached back into the fridge, the light from the flashlight positioned just right for him to make out the silhouette of her heart-shaped bottom jutting toward him. Her T-shirt had ridden up enough to reveal some skin and the little dimples in the small of her back. Did she even know what a temptation she presented him? His mouth went dry with the thought of running his fingers over what promised to be smooth-as-silk flesh.

He took a sudden step back. What in the world had come over him? Why was he suddenly looking at her as though she were one of the contenders for the date with him?

She turned around, shrimp tray in hand, and his breath caught with how beautiful she looked.

"What are you gawking at?" she asked him.

"I love shrimp." It was all he could think to say.

"We need to find the silverware and some plates." She glided past him and slid the tray onto the counter before snatching the flashlight from his hand and rummaging through the drawers and cabinets.

"The flashlight is fading fast," he said, opening a few drawers himself.

"Maybe we should grab the candelabra from the dining room just in case. One of the thousand drawers in here should have some matches or one of those lighter things."

"Okay, give me the flashlight, and stay put until I get back."

"Why can't I come with you?"

Because I need some time to get the image of your backside out of my head. He almost said it out loud. "Because I don't need you tripping and breaking something."

"'Kay."

Halfway out of the kitchen he stopped, turned, and shined the light on the tray. "And don't eat all the shrimp."

It seemed like Logan had only been gone two seconds when she heard him call out.

"Flashlight's dead."

"Can you find your way back here without tripping over something?" Freddy returned.

"Maybe. Keep talking. I'll try to retrace my steps exactly."

"What do you want me to say?"

"Whatever you'd like."

Whatever she'd like? Trying not to say what it was she would like proved to be harder than multiple choice on the SATs. She wanted to tell him that maybe they should bail out of this place before Ms. Perfect showed up tomorrow. Maybe instead they could try dating each other. And maybe if he wanted, he could kiss her now.

Yeah, and maybe the moon was really made of green cheese.

She thought about it for a minute more, but what came out of her mouth had nothing to do with what she actually thought.

"So what kind of woman are you looking for?"

She smacked the palm of her hand against her forehead and blamed it on nerves. She really did not want a detailed description of his perfect date.

"What?"

The single word hit her with the force of a category five hurricane. Bad enough she asked him, but now she would actually have to repeat the question. Or lie.

She opted for the lie.

"I asked what kind of candle you are looking for."

"No, you didn't. You asked what kind of woman I was looking for."

The voice was closer. She'd have to think fast.

"Did I? I meant candle."

"No, I believe you said 'woman,' not 'candle.'"

"Then why did you ask?"

His voice came from right in front of her now. "Because I didn't think I heard you right."

On the last word, his body slammed into hers, the contact knocking her off balance. Too far from the counter to reach back for support, she reached out and grabbed on to his shoulders to keep from falling instead. He responded by placing his hands on her hips. The lightning flashed, showing her his wide smile topped by half-lidded eyes.

"Oh," she muttered, trying to ignore the sheer pleasure of contact with his body. "I guess we really need that candle until the power comes on, after all."

"Maybe we don't have light." He backed her up until her backside touched the countertop. "But we can have some electricity of our own."

"How can you make jokes at a time like this?"

"What makes you think I'm joking?" His voice sounded husky to her.

He nuzzled her neck. "We're completely in the dark and at the mercy of the electricity gods. All we can do is feel our way around until the power comes back on." His hands moved to the rise of her back. "And, so far, I'm liking how it feels."

She felt his kiss on her cheek. Maybe the idea wasn't half-bad, she decided. *Carpe diem,* her mind screamed inside her head. And this time she would listen.

She just turned her head toward his kiss when, in the next flash of lightning, she thought she saw someone moving on the patio. Thinking it might be one of the production crew, she stiffened. As much as she had dreamed about being in Logan's arms, it suddenly felt staged, like a scene in a grade-B movie.

She pushed him away just as she heard a mechanical stutter and then the hum of the air conditioner and the ping of a light coming on—the power restored.

She looked up into his eyes and saw a whole other kind of power there. "I guess the transformer's working again."

"Bummer," he replied, holding her gaze but lowering his hands to his side.

Freddy recognized the uncomfortable body language. She pointed behind him. "I probably should go upstairs and clean up the glass."

She saw him lower his gaze to the floor before looking back at her. "And I should probably check outside." He started toward the double French doors leading outside and then stopped. "Want to come along?"

For a moment, she considered the invitation just to stay near him. But the storm had stopped. Both storms—the one outside and the one between them.

"No, I better get back to my room and clean up the glass before the power goes out again."

"If it does, stay put. I'll find you." Then he disappeared onto the patio.

She watched him until the landscape swallowed him, wondering all the time if she could short out the power again by jamming something into an outlet.

Darn, she wished she had paid more attention in science class sophomore year instead of passing notes to Patt.

"Holy crow, did you get it all?" Marty asked, punching the cameraman holding the infrared camera on the arm. "The bachelor and the evaluator in a lip-lock."

"They didn't kiss."

"A technicality. Nothing some creative editing won't fix." He grabbed the camera and rewound the video. "Look. You can't fit a piece of paper between them." He rewound it and played it again. "Right here we can fade to black, and let the audience draw their own conclusions."

"The picture is all green and kind of grainy," the camera tech commented.

"No one, especially the producer, will care about colors when we edit. The only question will be when to drop this bombshell during the series."

Marty and the cameraman looked at each other. "Sweeps week," they said in unison before high-fiving—topped with a chest bump for good measure.

Chapter Six

Logan shrugged and stretched his back, trying to shift the annoying feel of the microphone pack clipped to his belt under his tuxedo jacket. Hands clasped waist-level in front of him, he waited at the bottom of the marble steps of the front patio for the first of six limousines scheduled to arrive. Each one held a willing participant in what he could only describe as a reality version of an old matchmaking game show, one that would kick off when the first pair of high heels hit the driveway.

He looked at the sky a moment, gathering his thoughts. The situation did present some interesting possibilities, if he cared to take advantage of them. Six women, all handpicked out of thousands who applied, would be jockeying for his attention over the next few weeks. He imagined a list just as long of bachelors who would do just about anything to be in his shoes, a position even his wildest fantasies had not conjured.

He shifted again, the mike-pack bothering him even more than it had a few minutes ago. Not wanting the cameraman who stood about three feet from him to film him adjusting it, he jostled his shoulders again, getting the contraption to move just enough for it to be tolerable.

But the microphone wasn't the only thing bugging him. He glanced to his right to a balcony softly illuminated by light from the room behind it. He knew Freddy was there watching and waiting, too. He wondered if she felt as nervous as he did.

But the edge he felt did not just come because of the show. His strictly male reaction to Freddy had been a surprise—a very pleasant surprise.

He did not have a chance to talk to her about what almost happened between them in the kitchen during the blackout. The morning brought a flurry of activity: prep with the show's popular host, run-throughs, instructions on camera angles, lessons on the camera pack and mike, makeup, wardrobe, and whatever else the director thought to throw at them for the last twelve hours. He had no time to get Freddy alone and didn't think he would until the taping finally wrapped. But by then, if the show went as planned, he'd be on a ten-day date with one of the women winding up the long driveway in a stretch limo right now.

He might never know if his almost kiss with Freddy was genuine or something she had encouraged as part of the show.

And he had no time to think anymore about it, because the headlights of the first limo glimmered through the landscaping.

Showtime.

The camera tech on the balcony with Freddy pointed to her left. "The monitor is right there just out of camera range. You can see and hear everything happening in real time when Logan meets the bachelorettes. Can you see it okay?"

Freddy glanced at it. "It's fine."

A voice crackled in her ear. "I need a sound check. Give me a slow count."

Freddy pressed her forefinger onto the earpiece jammed in her left ear. "One, two, three..."

As she counted, she watched Logan. She could see him clearly. He looked great, a little nervous though. She couldn't blame him.

He was about to meet six women who knew he would be the ultimate prize in the love-game about to begin.

She looked at him again. Amid the extra lighting for taping, the strong angles of his jaw and curve of his lips were inviting. Any red-blooded woman would fall in love with him at first sight. No, not just any woman—every woman.

How was she ever going to get through the next few weeks, let alone pick out someone for him to take along on one incredible ten-day love fest?

"Try not to touch the earpiece during filming," the voice in her ear said, snapping her out of her reverie.

"Okay, but it's annoying."

"You'll get used to it."

Roberto came gliding on to the balcony, clipboard in hand. "Now, as the ladies arrive, we want you to watch Logan's reaction to them." His forefinger circled in the air, and Freddy turned in response to it. Roberto fiddled with her mike-pack and then traced the coiled wire coming from it to her earpiece. He smoothed her hair in front of it. "When the red light on the camera goes on," he pointed to the camera to show her where to look, "we'd like you to comment on what you see."

Freddy let out an exaggerated sigh. "Comment like how?"

"Be upbeat, chatty. Show the audience you're engaging in the process of choosing Logan's ultimate date."

Freddy's stomach dipped. She felt sick imaging what the women might look like. "What if I don't like them?"

Roberto looked surprised. "Why wouldn't you?" he said, rifling through the papers on his clipboard. "One's a beauty queen, we have a kindergarten teacher, a model, a..." he stopped talking and tilted his head, eyes cast upward, apparently listening to a voice in his earpiece. After a minute or so, he spun around and clapped his hands together. "People. Two minutes. The first car is almost here." As the crew scurried in response, he turned back to Freddy. "You'll have to find out about the rest of the ladies on the fly." Freddy heard him begin a count. "In five, four, three…" He gestured the last two numbers.

She had just enough time to look into the monitor and see Logan smile.

The limo driver walked to the rear passenger door and opened it. He extended his hand, and the woman inside took it. At first, Logan could only see the spiky heel of a gold shoe. Curiosity made him rise up slightly on his toes and lean forward. He smiled and made eye contact with the brunette who emerged.

Very attractive, he thought as she approached him. "Hi, I'm Logan."

"Stacy," she said, smiling back.

Her hand felt cold. "Nervous?"

"A little."

"I am, too." He covered her hand with his.

About the same time, a familiar voice crackled in his ear. *"Flirting already? You just met her."*

Logan knew Freddy would be joining him in the parlor once all the ladies arrived, but this came as a surprise. She could see and hear him as he greeted each one. She got him into this; now he had the chance to exact a little payback.

Purposely, he held on to Stacy's hand. "Welcome, Stacy. Tell me a little about yourself."

"Well, I'm from Morristown." She pointed over her shoulder with her free hand as Logan continued to hold the other. "That's just around the corner, and I teach kindergarten."

"Hope she didn't catch a cold or the flu from the little tykes. Maybe you should let go of her hand just in case."

He enjoyed hearing the edge in Freddy's voice. "I am looking forward to hearing more about that," he said to Stacy. "Why don't you go inside and get something to drink while we wait for the rest of the bachelorettes." He escorted her up the stairs to the front door, acutely aware Freddy watched his every move.

"Better save some charm, player. You do have five more women coming."

At the front door, he placed his hand on the small of Stacy's back and guided her inside. "See you soon." He almost laughed out loud when he heard Freddy let out a most unladylike snort. As he walked down the front steps to assume his place on the spot marked by the production crew, he looked up at the balcony where Freddy waited. With an exaggerated point, he gave her a "take that" gesture and a satisfied grin.

It might have backfired when her voice in his ear warned, *"Game on, Mr. Hunkadotious."*

Logan looked down at the ground and found his mark, easing onto it with a laugh. Maybe this would be fun after all.

"What are you doing?" Roberto threw open the French doors and joined Freddy on the balcony. "The director wants you to stop right now."

Freddy pasted on her most innocent smile. "I have no idea what you're talking about."

Roberto leaned over the balcony. "Cut!" he shouted, passing his hand back and forth in front of his neck.

Immediately, a buzz of voices rose, both from inside the room leading to the balcony and down on the area surrounding Logan. Makeup artists swooped in both places. On the balcony, one dabbed at the shiny spot on Freddy's nose while on the front courtyard, two draped cloths over Logan's tuxedo jacket, and a third used an airbrush to touch up the strong angle of his chin.

"He can hear everything you say," Roberto continued.

She dodged a hairbrush held by the stylist as it came toward her head. "I know that."

"So can I."

Freddy felt herself warm and hoped a blush wasn't creeping up her face. "I'm trying to keep him grounded."

"It's distracting. Stick to the script."

Freddy frowned. "I didn't read it."

Roberto's shoulders dropped in displeasure. "I left a script for the first show on the desk in your room. I expected you to read it."

Freddy grimaced when the stylist tugged on the hair extensions she'd placed at the back of Freddy's head earlier in the day. "Ow, quit it."

"Stay still," Roberto ordered. "On camera the lighting is showing a line between your hair and the extensions. We have to fix it. This is a high-def show and high-def shows no mercy."

"Then take it out. I didn't want prom-queen hair anyway."

Roberto pursed his lips in pique. "Too late. And it's not prom-queen hair, it's modern and uplifted." He looked her straight in the eye. "And in the contract."

"Okay." Freddy stopped fighting the stylist and let the stylist work. "But next time, not so much hair spray. I'm going to need a sandblaster to get it out."

"And I'll be happy to hold it for you." Roberto's smug tone left nothing to the imagination.

A technician poked his head out from inside the room, hand to his earpiece. "We're ready."

The crew scrambled back into the shadows as Roberto checked his clipboard. "Keep the comments to the minimum." He looked up. "We're rolling in five, four, three..." Again, he gestured the last two counts.

Freddy rolled her eyes and walked to the edge of the balcony. She gave the cameraman an exaggerated smile, indicating she was ready, and looked out at the driveway. In the distance, she could see the headlights of the second limo as it approached.

"I can't wait to see what gets out of this one," she muttered to herself, forgetting momentarily about the equipment attached to her back.

Roberto cleared his throat loudly, and when she looked at him, he made a zippering motion across his lips. She had no time to respond to the gesture because she heard the car pull up and the driver turn off the engine.

The next contestant had arrived.

Over the next twenty minutes, the five remaining participants arrived: Jade, a blonde model from the West Coast; Careelyn, a former Miss Southern States, who wore her ribbon from the beauty pageant; Lori, a redheaded nurse and Middle East veteran; Emily, who presented Logan with a poem she wrote about him; and Madison, a recent college graduate from the Northeast with a heavy Bostonian-type accent.

When the last one walked to the mansion on Logan's arm, Freddy ripped the earpiece from her ear. "You have got to be kidding me."

Roberto joined her on the balcony. "What's wrong now?"

"They brought props?"

"Maybe the pageant sash was a bit over the top."

"What about the poet? 'I think that I will never see, a girl as happy as me'?"

"You memorized it?"

Freddy pressed her palms to her eyes. "It's in my head like a Super Bowl commercial. You know the kind, no matter what, it keeps repeating."

Roberto looked pleased. "If that's what happens to the viewing audience, our ratings will go through the roof."

"So will visits to therapists."

"Whatever." Roberto pulled her by the arm from the balcony into the room. "Next we need to introduce you to the ladies and set down the ground rules for the next few weeks."

"Do they know about me?"

"Not exactly. We're going for the element of surprise as much as possible."

He signaled to a member of the production crew standing nearby. "Get her down to Annie. We begin shooting again in thirty minutes downstairs in the parlor," he pointed to Freddy, "and she needs a touch-up around her eyes."

As the bachelorettes were led out of the room, Logan turned when he heard Freddy's voice in the hall. He walked toward it, but froze when he saw her. She looked like an angel, her slim body accentuated to perfection by the silver gown she wore. Wisps of her auburn hair escaped the style imposed on her for the show and arched around her face in subtle but stubborn curls.

She seemed to be verbally sparring with Roberto, and Logan saw her swipe at the hands of the stylist who tried to tame the escaping curls. Remembering the many times they had been at odds over one thing or another through the years, he could not have stopped the smile that curved his lips if he wanted to. He'd lost many a battle on the opposite side of an issue from Freddy. She could be very tenacious when she wanted to be.

She began to spin in a circle to escape a comb when Roberto's stern voice seemed to stop her from dodging a makeup sponge. She gave Roberto an exaggerated cocked-hip pose and lifted her chin, holding perfectly still while the makeup artist dabbed at the area just underneath her eyes.

"Laugh it up, Logan," he heard her say. "You're next."

"I can't believe you're actually not moving," Logan tossed back. "Wish I knew this secret a long time ago. Instead of trying to pull a fancy move and get past you to score on the football field when we were kids, I'd have whipped out some Maybelline and froze you solid."

Freddy briefly turned her face to him. "The threat of mascara poking out the white of one's eyes does that to a person."

A few more people circled Freddy, and Logan had to be content to just look at her. She shifted and her dress simmered in the light, drawing his attention to the graceful arch of her hip. His gaze rose to her shoulders, bare except for two thin spaghetti straps.

The makeup artist brushed powder down her throat and across her décolleté, leaving a shimmer on her skin. As he looked at her, he felt his blood turn white hot in his veins. He sucked in a lungful of air to help cool the feeling. She looked incredible. Amazing. Like someone he wanted to touch.

The urge to do just that was so strong that he walked to a tray set up for the crew and curled one hand around a bottle of water. Why had he never noticed the woman in her like this before?

After a flurry of activity all around the room, the production crew left and she walked up to him. "Having fun yet?"

"Not as much as you."

"I watched you ogle every last one of the contestants."

"Aren't I supposed to get to know them before I pick one?"

"I'm picking your date," Freddy reminded. She looked over his shoulder. "Where are they anyway?"

"Somewhere getting a tune up like we did, I suppose." He leaned against an antique desk. "So which one did you like best so far?"

Freddy tapped a perfectly manicured finger onto her chin. "Let's see. Ms. Longfellow?"

"It was a nice poem."

Freddy rolled her eyes. "Please. I bet the kindergarten teacher heard better on writing day."

"You don't like her either?"

"She's okay."

Logan laughed. "I can tell by the tone of your voice."

"Seriously," Freddy continued. "What's her name was the best of the bunch."

"Stacy."

"Whatever."

Logan's grin grew wider. "If I didn't know better, I'd think you were jealous."

Freddy stared at him openmouthed for a few minutes. "Yeah, right." She raised her hand and waggled it back and forth in a kind of parade wave. "Miss Cotton Gin, or whatever she is, actually wore her sash."

"I thought it was kind of cute."

She dropped her hand to her side. "It made me want to barf. I took off points for that one."

"You're keeping score?"

"How else am I going to figure out which one wins?"

"So who is winning?"

Freddy scrunched up her nose as though a foul smell just moved by it. "Let's see, Miss Cotton Gin—two points, America's Next Top Model—two points, the poet—two points, Buffy…"

"Buffy?"

"Yeah, the preppie from Yale or Harvard or wherever Mummy and Daddy sent her—two points."

A smiled tugged at his mouth. "Anyone get more than two points?"

"The war veteran. She got an extra point because I'm patriotic. Three points."

"And Stacy?"

Freddy's brow furrowed. "You like her or something?"

Logan smiled at the indignant tone of Freddy's voice. She was jealous after all. "I might."

He saw something serious run across her face. She looked past him to the back of the room before returning her gaze to him. "She had four points, but I'm taking one point off right now."

"Why?"

"Because you…"

Roberto clapped his hands together. "Two minutes." He walked to Logan while scanning his clipboard bible. "Logan," he looked up just for a moment, "when this segment opens, you will be inside the parlor with the ladies. You'll have ten minutes to make the rounds, and let us get some shots of you socializing. Then the host will bring in Freddy and drop the bombshell that she is really the one to impress." He turned to Freddy. "Isn't that delicious?"

Freddy rolled her eyes. "Divine."

A production assistant began to lead Logan inside the parlor when he stopped and turned back. "What were you going to say before Roberto interrupted you?" He started to say something else, but the production assistant had already opened the connecting French doors, and the ladies surged toward it, their voices blending in a loud chorus of greeting.

Freddy watched as first one and then another ran to Logan's side when he stepped into the parlor, each one vying for position and attention. Soon beautiful women surrounded him, each one hanging on his every word. How could she ever compete?

She answered Logan's question in a whisper, grateful he would not be able to hear her. "Because I can tell you liked Stacy best. I took off a point just because you like her."

Chapter Seven

"Smile, we're on," the show's host said as he took her elbow. He led her inside the parlor. "Ladies, if you can tear yourself away from Logan for a moment, I will need your attention." Glasses clinked as they were set onto trays and everyone's attention moved to the show host. "This is Freddy," he continued. The collective intake of breath could have turned the room into a vacuum. "Freddy is playing an important role in the competition, so please listen carefully."

As the host revealed her part in the show, Freddy felt the weight of the gazes on her—some like daggers, some in shock.

"Now I'll give you all a few minutes to get acquainted."

Four of the women gave Freddy a quick sidelong glance before resuming their fixation on Logan. Lori, the war veteran, and Stacy, the teacher, homed right in on her.

Okay, it looks like the two smartest ones have this figured out, Freddy thought as they approached. *Guess that will make them among the first to go.*

"Interesting turn of events," Stacy said, holding out her hand to Freddy. "I'm Stacy."

Should I let her know I watched them all come in from the balcony? Freddy decided against it and took her hand. "Frederika." She shook Stacy's hand as warmly as possible, all the while picturing whipping Stacy into a headlock and body slamming her right into the pricey travertine tile in the entranceway.

"So Freddy is your nickname then?" Lori asked, not to be shut out of an opportunity to win Freddy over.

"Only for the show. I don't like it that much."

"Then Frederika it is," Lori announced. "Why don't we sit down somewhere quiet and you can get to know me better?" She pointed to a small patio to the right off a set of double French doors.

Not to be outdone, Stacy concurred. "Know *us* better, you mean. We can all get more comfortable with this new twist." She stepped between Stacy and Freddy. "I do like Frederika better. It sounds more elegant and regal." She smiled. "It suits you."

Gawd, Freddy thought. *She can't possibly think I am going to fall for that.*

Lori glanced over her shoulder. "But since the rest of the ladies haven't figured out that they should actually be putting their time to good use by getting to know the person who will be eliminating them, how about we don't tell them about it for a while?"

Freddy looked at the four remaining women circling Logan now like sharks about to partake in a feeding frenzy. "Why not," she agreed before looking at Stacy and Lori. *Trying to make alliances already, are you?* They were definitely going to be the first two with their butts in the backseat of limos heading back out the driveway. And as soon as possible.

What she didn't need were two beautiful *and* intelligent women in the mix. Suddenly, a pageant-waving beauty queen, a limerick-creating poet, a runway wannabe, and a New England preppie didn't seem too bad at all.

"I think that went rather well," Freddy said, entering Logan's room later that evening.

He came out of his dressing room wearing jeans and his tuxedo shirt, unbuttoned, both humor and questions in his eyes. "It depends on what you mean by 'went well.'"

"You looked like you enjoyed the attention," she said, pulling back hard on the reins of the female hormones raging inside her when she looked at him. Her fingertips itched to trace the six-pack abs peeking from beneath the crisp white fabric to find out if they were as rock hard as they looked. "Were you?"

"It wasn't half-bad." He lifted his carved-from-stone shoulders and shrugged off the shirt. "Hang on a second," he said before ducking back inside the dressing room.

Freddy grabbed on to the back of one of the overstuffed chairs to keep from running after him just to watch him put on a T-shirt.

"So what's next?" she heard him call out from the other room.

What's next? How was she supposed to answer that? She'd spent the better part of the last hour dodging elbows and trying to stay close to Logan as six women jockeyed for position next to him. Watching them shamelessly and openly flirt with him only underscored the fact that her great plan to impress him had taken a really wrong turn. The ladies would probably be wiping drool from their chins all night now that they had seen him, and she could do nothing more about it than hand them a tissue. She looked to the window, half-expecting to see one of the bachelorettes climbing on a ladder.

Logan came back into the room in a plain white T-shirt, looking more like the Logan she knew and less like a model on the cover of *GQ*. She leaned her rear against the desk in his room, slippers peeking out from beneath the silvery fabric of her gown. "Seems like I have a lot on the agenda. I have to go over the list of upcoming challenges and get my comments to Annie by Thursday. Two days. I hope you don't get too bored hanging around here with nothing to do but look at women in bikinis walk back and forth between the pool and the hot tub."

"I'm sure I can adjust."

She snickered. "You do that."

"What else can I do? You got me into this."

"Want out?" Her hopes soared.

"I think it's too late for that," he replied, dashing those hopes. "But I have to admit, as exciting this may all seems to the viewers, it's all beginning to run together in my head."

Suddenly, the evening sounded more interesting. "It is?" Freddy shifted her rear on the desk. "You don't like all the attention?"

"I do. I mean, what guy wouldn't want six beautiful hand-picked women fawning all over him?"

"I sense a 'but' coming."

He nodded. "But it doesn't feel real." He tossed his head toward the desk. "We have a script. How can anything be real if it is scripted?" Dismay darkened his eyes. "What if I make the wrong choice?"

"You won't."

"How can you be sure?"

"Because making the choice is my job."

He smiled. "That's right. It is." His eyes narrowed. "You won't let me down, will you?"

He turned his smile up a notch, and it seared into Freddy's heart as if it had touched the infrared grate on an outdoor grill. As she looked at the curve of his lips, all she could think about was someone else kissing him, someone to whom she would have to give the "go for it" seal of approval in six weeks. She wondered if she could actually do it.

"The producers tell me I have to give them a good show or risk being in default of the contract," she managed to say once she tore her gaze from his mouth.

"I just hope you have some sort of internal radar inside that head of yours to weed out the star-seekers from the genuine article."

Freddy suddenly found it hard to breathe. "You are actually looking for a girlfriend?"

Logan shrugged. "I dunno. Maybe."

Stunned, Freddy could only stare openmouthed at him.

"I am stuck here, so maybe I should try to make the best of things. I mean, I would never have met women like this if it hadn't been for you entering my picture in the contest. I tend to stick to the same type of girl."

"And what type would that be?" she asked in a small voice.

He tilted his head and shook his finger at her. "Oh, no you don't."

"Don't what?"

"You don't actually think I'm going to spell it out for you."

"Why not?"

"Because if I do, you won't have as much work to do over the next few weeks. I think I would like to be entertained as long as I have to be here, and watching you figure out who stays and who goes could turn out to be a lot of fun."

"Fun? It was like auction day at Christie's, and you were up for bidding like a piece of art or something."

Logan flexed his bicep. "I am fine." He couldn't stop the laughter. "But seriously. We've known each other a long time. You know me, know what I like."

She *so* did not want to go down this road with him because that particular road did not lead to her.

"Besides," he continued, "if I tell you, what will you do with the points? Your scoring system would get out of whack."

"Not to me."

He took a step toward her and tucked a lock of her hair behind her ear with his forefinger. "Tell you what. Forget the points, and just do what feels right," he said with a wry smile.

What felt right to her would be running for the hills with Logan in tow. There had to be a way out of this. She just needed time to find it. "As long as you let me do what I'm supposed to do and not fight me on any decision, I promise you that when I'm done, you'll be happy."

"Sounds like you're already on track."

She shook her head. "No. I'm not. I'm making this up as I go along. It would be a heck of a lot easier if I did have a Goth girl or the stereotypical biker chick here, but I don't, so it makes my job a lot harder."

He raised an eyebrow. "You'd pick one of those for me?"

"Yep."

"Why?"

"Ratings," she said before walking to the door where she stopped and turned back to face him. "Don't stay up too late. Tomorrow is the first group date, and you're going to need all the rest you can get."

Chapter Eight

"Where are we going?" Logan asked, getting into the waiting limo and finding Freddy already there.

"It's a surprise."

The car took off. "Where are my dates?"

"Probably already at the site."

"Site of what?"

"Your group date."

The quirk on her lips gave her away. He wasn't getting any information until they got to wherever they were going. He reached into the small fridge and pulled out a bottled water. "What's up with all the secrecy? Why won't you tell me what's planned?" He took a long swig, waiting for her answer.

"Hand me one," Freddy asked, reaching out.

Logan grabbed her wrist. "Not until you tell me what's going on. The note that came with the breakfast tray this morning just said dress for sports. Are we playing football?"

"Not this time, but it is a thought."

He let her wrist go and got the water she wanted. "If you want me to teach six beautiful women how to tackle, I'm in."

"I think I can handle that, remember? But not today."

"So why won't you tell me where we are going?" He raked her with a look, taking in her T-shirt, jeans, and sturdy brown shoes that were a cross between sneakers and hiking boots. Her hair was back in a ponytail, and she had on the barest amount of makeup—some mascara and pink lip gloss that made her mouth look amazing. She didn't need all the makeup the artists put on her last night. She looked equally as great this morning without it. "If not football, then what?"

Freddy shrugged. "I guess it couldn't hurt to tell you. We're almost there anyway. We're all going to play a little game of elimination paintball. Last one standing gets a one-on-one date with you tomorrow."

As promised, the women were already at the paintball field when Freddy and Logan arrived. The show's host stepped forward, and a secondary set of cameras began to roll, augmenting the ones that filmed Freddy and Logan pulling up and getting out of the limo.

"As you can see," the host began, "the ladies are already dressed and ready to play." He gestured to two young men dressed in uniforms who handed Freddy and Logan some camouflage pants and jackets, along with the required safety masks and goggles. "Put these on, and I'll explain the rules."

As everyone gathered around the host, he began. "Basically, this will be a game of teamwork and strategy. Logan and Freddy and one of the professional team players will have the show's flag." He reached down and picked up a triangle-shaped red flag with a large white heart in the center. He handed it to Logan. "The other professional will join the bachelorettes. The ladies will have to find and capture the flag while Logan and Freddy try to make sure that doesn't happen."

Freddy raised her mask so she could talk. "Not counting the professionals, aren't we outmanned six to two here?"

The show host laughed. "Only one of the ladies can claim the flag. They'll have to use both teamwork to find it and strategy to be the last one standing."

"So we can shoot them, and they can shoot each other," Freddy reasoned aloud.

"If that's the strategy they decide to use. But ultimately, the one with the flag at the end of the day wins the date with Logan."

Freddy pointed to Logan. "And he can eliminate anyone he wants by shooting them also, right?"

"Or he can show any of them where the flag is if he wants to spend more time with one of the contestants."

Freddy snapped her head toward Logan. She couldn't see much of him with the mask and goggles he wore, but she could see his eyes were crinkled in a smile. She took the flag from his hand. "I'll take that."

Logan's eyes crinkled even more.

"Now I'll let Max and Jerry, the professional paintball players, give out the rest of the equipment and explain the rules."

"Cut!" Roberto appeared from behind one of the shelters. "We don't need to shoot the boring stuff. We'll pick it up once everyone is in place for the game to start." He wore what could only be described as a seventies warm-up suit in dark blue fabric with white stripes down the sides of the pants.

"Borrow that from your grandfather?" Freddy asked when Roberto was next to her.

"Dolce and Gabbana," he said, snapping his fingers to show his disapproval. He looked her camouflage pants and jacket up and down. "Very G. I. Jane."

"Hooah," she replied.

Logan handed her one of the paintball guns. "Listen up, or you'll be the first to go."

Everyone crowded around the professional paintball players and listened. Max then held up his paintball shooter.

"I don't like guns or war," Stacy said instantly.

"We don't call it a gun, we call it a marker. This isn't war. It's a game." Max continued, pointing as he spoke. "This is the hopper on top. It holds one hundred paintballs and the compressed air bottle here for propellant." He took some paintballs from his pockets. "Anybody play before?"

Freddy raised her hand.

"You never played," Logan whispered to her.

"How would you know? You're always working." She raised her voice. "Three times."

Max held out his hand, the paintballs in his palm. "So then you know these are carbowax with some other nontoxic, water-soluble stuff and dye, and while they are soft enough," he squeezed one between his thumb and forefinger, "they can hurt like the dickens if you get gogged or shot point-blank."

"Gogged?" one of the ladies asked.

"Getting hit in the goggles as opposed to 'eating paint,' which is getting shot in the mask. So no shooting at anyone's head. Being marked, or shot by a paintball, can leave a welt at close distances."

"So if anyone gets marked, they are out?" Freddy asked.

"Yeah. And 'wiping' is an automatic disqual. That's when you attempt to remove the spot where you were marked. But a bounce is legal, and you can stay in the game."

"Define 'bounce,'" Freddy said.

"It's when a paintball hits a player but does not break." He pointed to his partner. "Jerry will take the ladies back to the far edge of the field beyond the woods, and we'll find a place to protect the flag."

Everyone moved to join their teams.

"Stay inside the base for now." Max gestured to the large rectangle they stood inside, outlined with red landscaping paint. "Once we start, and you're outside the base, anything goes. A few more things. If you get tagged, you raise your marker over your head to signify that you're out and move straight to the dead box." He pointed to a second red-outlined rectangle at the edge of the field. "That's it over there. When you're hit, you get there and stay there until the match is over. And do not give in to the urge to shoot anyone coming by." He nodded to Jerry and then turned. "Everyone ready?"

Cheers went up from the women.

"Then let's play some paintball."

They all began to walk away from the base when Jade's marker went off, shooting a paintball straight onto the ground. She shrieked in surprise as dirt rose from the dry ground around her. "Sorry," she said, "my bad."

Jerry started toward her when Lori waved him off. "I got this," she said and then proceeded to instruct Jade on how to shoot, along with proper safety measures.

"Hey," Freddy called out. "You've played before?"

Lori shook her head and continued to help Jade.

"She's army. She knows how to shoot," Logan reminded Freddy.

Freddy nodded. "Oh yeah. I almost forgot."

Once the instruction was over, Max raised his hand. "Let's try this again. Ready? Game on!" The ladies shouted in delight and began walking off with him to their starting point.

Freddy looked down at the ground. "The game is on now, right?" Max nodded. She dropped to one knee, pretending to tie her shoe. "You two go ahead, I'll catch up."

"You sure?" Logan asked.

"I'm a minute behind you."

She watched them walk off, and once they were out of sight, she took off running in the direction the women had taken.

She had no trouble finding them. Their laughing and chattering like chipmunks made them all pretty noisy targets. Staying back enough for her not to be heard, she tested her paintball marker on a tree, hitting it with three shots. At least now she knew what it felt like to fire it. Then she approached the ladies as quietly as possible. To her luck, Lori was last in line as they followed a pathway. Perfect, because the war vet had to go first.

Taking aim at Lori's rear, Freddy got off four quick shots, two of them hitting the mark. "You're out, soldier-lady," Freddy shouted before turning and running off as fast as she could, hearing paintballs fall well short of her retreat as the women fired back at her.

So much for the marksman, she thought triumphantly as she sped off to find Logan at the opposite end of the course. One down, five more to go. No one was capturing Logan's flag today if she could help it.

Freddy peeked around the side of the structure in which she had hidden the flag. About eight feet high and ten feet wide, it was basically a box with a three-foot-square opening in front. It had been peppered with paintballs over the years, giving it a psychedelic eighties feel.

"Do you see anyone?" Logan asked. He dropped to one knee beside her, paintball gun in hand.

Freddy suddenly let out a few blasts from her gun, the paintballs hitting the small bushes across the way. From the underbrush, a rabbit scampered away, apparently scared, but not hit.

"Nice shooting, ace," Logan quipped, seeing a blue spot on the rabbit's side.

Freddy laughed. "Guess he's on his way to the dead box."

Logan stood and took off his mask and goggles. "We've been out here for two hours already, and not an opponent in sight. Our pro has disappeared, too. What do you say we take a break?"

Freddy shook her head. "What if someone gets the flag?"

Logan turned in a circle, one hand out, one hand gripping the paintball marker. "No one's here."

A small rivulet of perspiration ran down his cheek. It was hot in the getup they wore. Maybe a fifteen-minute break wouldn't hurt, she decided. "Okay, but inside this box thing. I don't want to be ambushed."

Logan signed to the camera crew following them that they were going inside. "How can anyone hide with a shoulder cam and boom mike following them around?"

"We're not supposed to hide," Freddy said, ducking inside. "We're supposed to give good TV."

They sat down, leaning against the back wall. Freddy slid off her mask and goggles and set them down. "This is cozy."

Logan didn't agree. "If you like hot, humid boxes. You'd better hope no one comes up on us. We're sitting ducks."

"My strategy exactly. Since I eliminated the soldier, no one will think to look in here. Too obvious."

"When did you eliminate Lori?"

"Before I got here. She would have aced this course. Couldn't have that."

"Ah, so that's why you were tying laces that didn't exist on your shoes."

Freddy looked down at her feet. "Didn't think you'd notice shoes unless there were three-inch stiletto heels attached."

Logan winked. "I notice a lot of things."

But not me, Freddy thought.

"Why the long face?" Logan asked.

She shrugged. "This isn't coming out the way I thought it would."

"And what way was that?"

Now's your chance. Tell him. But she couldn't seem to do it. Instead, she looked around the bunker. "Oh, I don't know, sitting here waiting to pick off your girlfriends one at a time isn't really the way I thought I'd spend the day."

"They're not my girlfriends."

"They think so."

Logan laughed. "It is an odd situation."

She angled her eyes toward him, but said nothing.

He arched an arm around her shoulders. "Hey. C'mon. It's not so bad. We get to spend sometime alone in here away from the cameras. And at least we don't have to wear the mike-packs because of the face masks."

"That is a good thing," she agreed. Especially because with some creative editing, anything they said could wind up on the show, and she wanted to say a lot to him right now.

She burrowed into him as much as she could without having it feel too cozy, but enough for it to feel like heaven to her. His strong arm felt solid across her back, and she could feel his warmth seep into her.

She turned just enough to gaze up at him, and the contentment she saw in his eyes struck her as though someone hit her with a concrete block. He held out his hand, and she resisted the urge to tangle her fingers with his. Instead, she placed her marker in his palm. He turned and set it against the wall, but his arm stayed around her shoulders.

"Maybe we should stay armed," she said, "in case someone sneaks up on us."

"We have to end this game sometime. I'd rather get the first date over with."

She straightened. "You're in a hurry or something?"

"Maybe. I haven't dated anyone in a while. It might feel good to get back into the game."

"Glad I could help with that." She tried to dilute the sarcasm in her voice, but knew it still encased her words.

He pulled her back to him, and she didn't resist. "This was your idea, and there seems to be no way out until it's over."

She sighed. "I guess not."

"Second thoughts?"

"And third and fourth."

He cocked an eyebrow at her. "You were always the impulsive type."

"How would you know? You haven't paid much attention to me."

"And how would you know that?"

"Because I pay attention."

"Is that so?"

She nodded, enjoying the rock-hard solidness of his shoulder. Her heart ached with the thought of one of the other women enjoying the same feeling if she let them into the circle of his arms. And she died a little inside knowing she would have to put one of them there.

When his fingers started to move up and down her arm, she could hardly breathe. "Stop that."

"Stop what."

"Scratching my arm."

Immediately, he complied and took his arm away. "Sorry. I didn't realize I was annoying you."

She looked into his incredible eyes. "You weren't. It felt kind of nice."

As soon as the words left her mouth, her chest tightened in alarm. What on earth possessed her? She had no business saying things like that. In a few weeks, they would be on national TV—he as the world's most eligible bachelor, she as the world's most inept yenta, or at least that's how she'd describe herself now. Yentas did not feel the way she felt sitting next to Logan. Yentas did not try to figure how to be the *yentee*.

This was bad, really bad. Spending time alone with him made her hormones race, flipping all her feminine switches to the *on* position.

"Are you saying that you like me holding you?" she heard him ask. His voice seemed to be coming from somewhere in another time zone, and she had to shake her head to register what he said.

She was sure her face showed all the shock that settled inside her once she realized he wanted her to answer the question. Her mind screamed, *Yes*, but she made a face as though he had said the most ridiculous thing in the world. "No. I had an itch." One that was getting larger and harder to ignore.

"Okay then, because I would hate to have the camera catch that and have America misconstrue what's going on here."

Freddy's heartbeat rose. "There is nothing going on here."

He leaned closer to her. "Too bad."

"What—what did you say?"

"We could give this TV show a real twist if we wanted to." He leaned closer to her. "Where do you think the cameras are?" he whispered.

She could feel his hot breath on her skin. "Don't do that," she said. "Do what?"

He meant to tease her, and she knew it. But he couldn't know what his nearness was doing to her.

"Don't tempt me," she managed to stammer. But he was doing much more than that. His lips, so close to hers now, were just begging for her to lean in and…

She felt something hit her in the arm. It stung.

"Got you!" a distinctive female voice said, right before Jade ducked inside the bunker.

Freddy looked at Jade for a second before looking at her arm. No paint. It was a bouncer. She grabbed her marker, pulled the trigger, and fired off a few shots. "No, I believe I got you, missy." The paintballs splattered on Jade's breastplate shield, making a graffiti pattern. "You should have made sure your round broke," she said, right before scrambling to her feet and getting off a few more shots for good measure.

Jade dropped her marker. She held her hands out to the side. "I feel icky."

Freddy grabbed the marker from the ground. "You can clean up in the dead zone."

"A little overkill, don't you think?" Logan asked, rising and walking to Jade. "Are you okay?"

Jade nodded.

Freddy turned toward Logan. "Whose side are you on?"

"One shot would have been enough, Freddy."

"Oh, you mean like this one?" she asked before taking aim and plastering Logan with a shot.

"You can't shoot me," Logan exclaimed, raising his own marker and just missing Freddy's back as she grabbed the flag from its hiding place and ducked outside the bunker. "We're on the same side!"

"Not anymore," Freddy shouted before disappearing into the underbrush.

She ran until she was sure no one was following her, pleased with herself for a fraction of a second before she realized she had left Logan alone in a cozy bunker with Jade. She leaned against a tree and inhaled deeply to calm her racing heart, not knowing if the rise was due to her run or the situation in which she had left Logan.

Either way, it seemed she was way out of practice with this dating stuff.

Chapter Nine

A few hours later, Freddy stepped into the clearing and stared at a production set that could have been a postcard for the Bahamas. A large, brightly colored tent sat on what should have been the dead zone. Inside, she could see Logan lounging on a chaise and at least four of the ladies inside the tent with him. Tired and covered with a combination of dirt, leaves, and some goo she stepped in about a half mile back, she stormed right to it.

"I've been out there dodging wild animals and stepping in Lord knows what, and you sit here sipping umbrella-laden drinks in a cabana?" She pointed to the glass in his hand.

"I don't see an umbrella in anyone's glass," Logan countered.

"It's champagne," Jade volunteered.

Freddy glared at Jade. "Whatever." She turned back to Logan. "How long have you been here while I've been in what amounts to Seal training on the paintball course?"

A few of the ladies looked at her and snickered. Logan laughed. "Your own fault."

"How so?"

"If you'd bothered to count, you would have figured out that you shot everyone hours ago." As if on cue, the ladies stood and presented the parts of them hit by paintballs from Freddy's marker. Logan stood and walked to Jade, pointing. "She took about twenty of your shots, mostly to the breastplate protector, but one got her arm." Jade beamed in response.

"That's one," Freddy conceded.

One by one, Logan pointed out smears of paint. "Leg, shoulder, thigh, calf, and poor Lori," he waited until she turned her back to them, "the cruelest shot of all, her butt."

Freddy felt herself fuming as Lori rocked her hips back and forth, the yellow splotch on her backside dancing with the movement.

"That makes six." Logan's face suddenly beamed with a look that could only be described as pure satisfaction. "No, I mean seven. You actually shot me, too." He arched his arms around the two ladies closest to him. "I suppose that means I get to date everyone."

Freddy corralled the urge to empty the rest of the paintballs loaded in her marker right into him. She turned on her heel and started walking away.

"Where are you going?" Logan called out just as she passed Roberto walking toward her.

"Back to the mansion," she called back.

Roberto stopped her. "You can't."

"Why not?"

"Because we have to reshoot. You have to let someone get the flag."

"No, I don't," Freddy countered.

Roberto reached into the briefcase he always carried and pulled out the script. "Yes, you do. It says right here, whoever has the flag gets the one-on-one date with Logan."

"Let me see that," Freddy insisted.

Roberto angled the paper toward her. Freddy raised her marker and dotted the paper with five shots dead center. "Sorry, can't read it. There seems to be paint smudges across the writing."

Stunned, Roberto watched her storm off into the woods before he could say another word. He turned toward Logan, openmouthed.

"Sorry, can't help you with this one," Logan said, laughing. "You'll just have to figure out some sort of alternate end to the first episode."

"But the script says the person who has the flag gets the date."

"I guess by the rules that would be Freddy then."

Roberto shook his head. "The executive producer isn't going to be happy about this."

Logan saw the last bit of Freddy disappear behind a clump of trees. "It doesn't seem that Freddy is either."

Roberto signaled to one of the production crew members. "You. Go get her. We have an elimination ceremony in two hours, and she needs to get back to the mansion for hair and makeup."

Logan chuckled. "You should make her walk back and then go on camera in her paintball-spattered stuff. It would serve her right."

Back at the mansion, Freddy shut the door to her room and pulled the red flag from her back pocket. In a fit of temper, she'd outsmarted herself by shooting everyone, including Logan, with the paintball marker. When Roberto caught up to her on the way back to the mansion, he informed her that because of her actions, she would have to hand the flag to one of the six ladies tonight for a one-on-one date with Logan the next day, as well as eliminate one of them. The elimination she could do—handing Logan over to one of the bachelorettes, not so much.

She walked to the bathroom, and for a brief moment, thought about flushing the flag down the toilet. But that would change nothing. In the morning, someone would be spending the day with Logan, and it wasn't going to be her.

Or could it? Maybe she would just set Mr. Roberto back on the heels of his brown leather Berlutis and announce to the world once they were filming that she would be Logan's date for the evening. If nothing else, it would make for good TV.

She blew out a deep breath. She couldn't do that. This show could put Logan's ad agency in a whole other marketing class, and maybe set him on the path to becoming a full partner. He talked about that a lot during the monthly get-togethers with their friends, especially lately since a junior partnership dangled within his grasp. He deserved the chance, and she could help give it to him.

A knock at the door stopped her anguish for the moment.

"Freddy?"

Logan. She needed no more torture today. She stayed perfectly still, hoping he'd go away.

He knocked again. "Fred. I know you're in there. Roberto told me. Open up. I want to talk to you."

She guessed she had no choice. "What do you want?" she asked after opening the door.

Logan had a sandwich and two vitamin water drinks on the tray he held with one hand. "I thought you might be hungry."

She looked at the food. "Turkey?"

He smiled. "You talking about me or the sandwich?"

She smirked. "Take your pick."

"It's chicken."

"I guess I could eat." She stepped back. "Put it on the desk."

"They're not both for you."

"Didn't you fill up on the food in the cabana at the paintball field?"

He shook his head as he slid the tray onto the mahogany desktop like a peace offering. "Naw. Every time I tried to eat something, one of the ladies would ask me a question. It would have been rude to talk with my mouth full."

"I suppose."

He took one of the waters and walked to the leather couch against the wall across the room. After tossing one of the throw pillows against the armrest, he lay down and set the bottle on the floor. Stretched out across the sofa cushions, he took up the whole length of the couch.

Arms crossed, Freddy walked to a chair opposite him and sat. "Comfortable?"

He snuggled deeper into the deep brown leather. "Very." He shifted to his side and propped his head up with one hand. "You didn't get my message?"

The position accentuated his long lean lines. It didn't help one bit that a lock of hair had fallen over one eye. "And what message would that be?"

"I asked Roberto to tell you I'd be in the pool if you wanted to join me."

"How many of the ladies were in the water with you?"

"Three."

She shook her head. "No, thanks. Not even at gunpoint."

"I thought you might want to get to know some of them better, considering you have to pick one for me tonight."

He smiled at her, and she pictured her hand squishing the grin right off his face. "I've already picked one," she lied.

"Care to tell me who?"

"Nope." She stood. Maybe for emphasis, she didn't know.

"Come on, Fred. You tell me your plans, and I'll tell you mine."

"Your plans for what?"

"The date. Roberto left it up to me."

"How about you go first, and lay it all out for me," she said with a flourish of her arms.

"All of it?"

"Every gruesome detail."

Logan sat up. "Okay, I'll play along. I thought we'd do a little shopping on Main Street in Morristown first. Maybe I'll buy a bunch of flowers so my date can press one in a book."

"Right next to the prom corsage, I suppose," Freddy snapped, wrinkling her nose.

He ignored the barb. "Then we'd have dinner in one of the little restaurants on a side street, a cozy, out-of-the-way local place. Then perhaps a midnight walk in the park with our shoes off. I'll carry both pairs, of course." He smiled as if in victory. "Good plan, huh?"

Freddy found it hard not to have imagined herself as the woman on his arm in the park with her shoes off. "Depends. Sounds a bit sugary-sweet to me."

"You're saying I'm not sweet?"

She dismissed the question with a swipe of her hand. "Yes. Right. Sweet like syrup. And knowing that, I have to factor in everything I know about you, your flaws, your weaknesses, and such, in order to match you up with someone who won't take advantage of you."

Logan furrowed his brows. "I have weaknesses?"

"Several."

"Like what?"

"Look at the date you planned. You're a moosh. If one of those banshees figures it out, you're a sob story away from proposing."

"Banshees?"

"Ladies. Whatever. You know what I mean."

"Don't think so."

Freddy rolled her eyes. "I've known you since you were twelve. You asked nerds to dance during prom just because you felt sorry for them." She snapped her head more fully toward him. "Do you know you never asked me to dance once?"

His eyebrows rose. "I didn't?"

"Not once."

"You weren't a nerd."

"Nice of you to notice."

"You should have told me that you wanted to dance with me."

"I didn't think I had to."

"I guess I'm not that great of a catch, so you don't have to worry about the date."

"Who said I'm worried?"

He stood and walked to her, then reached out and brushed the hair from her face. "I can see it in your eyes."

She shrugged his hand away and sat back down. "I just don't want someone to try to take advantage of the situation tomorrow night after having to endure a whole day with you."

He smirked. "You mean take advantage of the moonlight."

"It will not be moonlight in your face. It will be the camera lights."

"Still." He waggled his eyebrows up and down. "It could be very romantic."

"I suppose, if you discount the millions of TV viewers who will be along on the date with you."

"There is that."

"So how romantic can it possibly be with all those eyes on you?"

He went back to the sofa and shifted to a position that looked like it belonged on a shrink's couch. Reaching down, he twisted the bottle on the floor casually with one hand, a faraway look on his face. Then he glanced at Freddy through a fallen strand of hair. "Don't be so sure about that. My date may forget all about the TV viewers. I can be very distracting. I believe you saw just how much when the lights went out the other day."

Freddy swallowed hard. Logan in the dark had been über-distracting. She distinctly remembered his eyes reflecting every bit of lightning they captured, his lips looking full and ready to kiss in the shadows playing off his face. A feeling of weight building inside her chest made her breathe hard and deep, as all her feminine synapses tuned into him.

She squared her shoulders. "It won't be the same. We were alone in this huge place."

"You were concentrating on the blackout, and I got your mind off it." He tapped his lips with his forefinger. "If I remember correctly. I would call that pretty distracting. Suddenly, you seemed to forget that you signed an iron-clad contract to hook me up at the end of this adventure."

Heat started to grow inside her, and she wondered if it showed on the apples of her cheeks, which burned as if they were seven inches from the sun. "Maybe you got close to kissing me, but I was nowhere near there." She walked away from him.

"Is that so?" He tapped a forefinger on his chin. "Hmmm. Could have fooled me."

"So you better get that notion out of your mind and concentrate on what's ahead of you," she said, hoping her voice sounded unemotional. "Because tomorrow, one lady gets you all to herself for a few hours, and it's up to me which one."

He turned to look at her. "You want a hint on which one I'd like?"

"No," she said quickly. "But I promise this will be a positive experience if we stick to the plan."

He pulled himself up and stood. "You never got around to telling me what the plan actually was."

She smiled. "I guess that means I distracted you."

"I guess you did." He walked to her and parked one hip dangerously close to her before crossing his arms and looking down.

She leaned back in the chair to put as much distance between them as she could. His nearness was making it a little hard for her to concentrate. "Ready to hear my plan?" she managed to whisper after looking up into his incredible eyes.

"I don't know. Am I?" He put his hands on the armrests, virtually locking her in place.

She closed her fingers around the seat and looked up at him. "We can team up right now, outsmart Roberto, and have a whole lot of fun in the process."

"What's the catch?"

"I'll pick the date; you keep it platonic."

He straightened, a puzzled expression on his face. "How does that make it fun for me?"

"I'm sure word will spread among the women like proverbial wildfire. Each one will ramp up the interaction. Won't it be fun to see what they do while you stay at arm's length from them?" Lordy, she hoped she sounded convincing. She watched plenty of reality TV love shows. There was no other way she could think of to keep his lips off theirs and vice versa.

"I'm not sure that will work," he said, straightening and sounding quite serious.

Freddy's stomach lurched. "Why?"

"Won't make good TV. There are always hugs and hand-holding and kisses. Why should my show be any different?"

"It's your show now? A bit arrogant, don't you think?"

"Well, it is called *Eligible Bachelor*, not *Blindside Your Best Friend*."

"So that's what this is all about. You're still mad at me for getting you into this."

"Trapping me into this," he corrected.

She flipped her hand. "Whatever."

As if she had also flipped his angry switch to full-on, Logan grabbed the armrests again and pinned her to the chair's backrest with his gaze. "It's whatever it takes to get me through this little game and back to work."

Freddy pressed herself as deeply into the woven fabric as the backrest would allow. Logan's face loomed about two inches from hers. "Exactly what do you mean?"

"I mean I will play this game out and be darn entertaining about it because I don't have a choice. If I don't give good, convincing TV, then how can I possibly sell ad campaigns to clients? How effective does bombing in the ratings make me look for realistic marketing pitches?"

Freddy grimaced. "I'll have to think about that."

"And while you're thinking about the corner you put me into, you can also think about this." He closed the small space between them and kissed her.

As his lips closed over hers, she managed a small intake of breath. It didn't take long for the blood to rush to her head and pound in her ears. His lips were warm and soft. They tasted like good wine—rich, spicy, with maybe a hint of boldness—and she wanted to taste a bit more. So she did the only thing she could think to do under the circumstances: she grabbed his shoulders and kissed him back.

She didn't know when he'd pulled her to her feet or when he had put his arms around her. But suddenly, they were wrapped around each other, kissing with every ounce of passion they could muster.

How long the kisses lasted, she didn't know that either, only that it had not been nearly long enough when he took his mouth from hers far enough to speak. "Well, this is a development the producers won't see coming."

"What do you mean?"

"I felt the way you kissed me back, Freddy. You can't want me to kiss anyone else."

He was right, so terribly right. She didn't want him to kiss anyone else; she wanted him to kiss her and only her. Already well into the show, doing anything but fulfilling the contract she signed—albeit without reading it—would have serious consequences for Logan and his job. She had no choice but to finish what she started, no matter how much she hated the thought.

Her head swam from the kiss, but somehow she managed to clear the fog enough to speak. "It doesn't matter much what either of us wants. It only matters about a signed contract with heavy-duty penalty clauses if either of us tries to break it."

"Then you want me to kiss other women."

"You know it's not that simple anymore. The show's filming. A lot of money has already been spent, money for the mansion, money to bring everyone here. And let's not even mention the food and wardrobe bill for the cast and production staff. I bet it's astronomical already. Have you seen the size of the key grips alone?"

"So it boils down to appearances and protocols?"

She shrugged. "What else could it be?" Had her face stayed neutral? Gawd, she hoped so because her insides were reeling.

"Okay." He straightened and the warmth that bubbled between them dissipated, as fast as she imagined an ice cube probably would melt on Venus.

"Okay," she repeated.

The ensuing silence roared, broken mercifully in a few moments by a chorus of voices in the hallway. Freddy looked over Logan's shoulder toward the din. A large gang of people gathered in the hallway.

A woman with big hair and even bigger eyeliner pushed her way into the room. "We have two hours for hair and makeup." She walked to Freddy and ran a hand through Freddy's hair. "And I think we'll need every minute of it." She turned to Logan and made a dismissing gesture. "So if you wouldn't mind, I believe someone is laying out wardrobe for you in your suite."

As three people surrounded her, Freddy watched Logan leave. Her heart sank deeper into her stomach. Someone pushed a chair right behind her knees, and she fell into it. She felt hairbrushes tangle into her hair.

"And this is the dress for tonight, people," she heard Roberto say. Out of the corner of her eye, she could see a flash of blue she had never seen on any color wheel. The dress hung from a satin hanger and looked ridiculously soft with the way it poured to the floor in graceful curves.

The makeup artist opened a huge train case and began mixing colors to match it. "Don't worry, honey," he said, setting out more brushes than Michelangelo would have used painting the Sistine Chapel. "I promise you're not going to recognize yourself after I'm done with you."

That's good, Freddy thought—because when she watched the show when it aired in a few weeks, she'd rather think someone else handed Logan over to another woman for the day.

Chapter Ten

Logan rubbed the back of his neck, trying to shake the headache that came on suddenly, almost dislodging the earpiece in his left ear.

"Remember to keep the left side of your body out of the camera angles as much as possible to hide the earpiece," Roberto's cautioning voice said. "If there seems to be a lull in the action, I'll prompt you with something to do to pick up the pace."

Logan shot Roberto a thumbs-up just as Emily approached.

She handed him a folded bit of paper. "I wrote this for you."

"Another poem?" he asked, taking it from her hand.

She nodded. "I've decided to write a poem about each experience we have and then post them all on Facebook after this is over."

Logan heard a loud sigh over the earpiece, right before Freddy's voice. *"Oh, she is so out of here."*

He turned his head and feigned a cough to cover what would have been a laugh.

"Are you all right?" Emily asked him, touching his shoulder.

Logan smiled as he turned to her. "Nothing more than an annoying little irritation that pops up from time to time."

"Let me get you some water," Emily said, spinning on her heels.

"Annoying irritation?" Freddy's voice crackled in his ear.

Logan put his fingertips on the earpiece. "That about describes it."

"What does the poem say this time?"

He unfolded the paper and read. "Something about the adventure of the chase and the spoils of war."

"Something about that or exactly about that."

He ignored the brevity in her tone. "And about how nice it would be to walk through the woods in the moonlight with me."

"Good thing she's a writer because she can use her imagination for that one. She is so gone."

"You can't toss her off the show just because she wrote me a poem."

"Watch me."

Logan tapped the earpiece. "What was that? You're breaking up."

Freddy started yelling—loud and nearly unintelligible because she talked so fast. Logan coughed again to cover a laugh and took the earpiece out, letting it hang over his shoulder. Every now and then, he'd lift the earpiece from his shoulder and angle it toward his ear. He could still hear Freddy yelling.

"Now what's wrong?" Roberto asked, watching Freddy pace inside the library.

She stopped and turned slowly to him, pointing in the direction of the study. "That is the most infuriating man ever."

Roberto looked pleased. "Perfect. Makes for good TV."

She rolled her eyes, the universal sign of annoyance. "I hate it when you say that."

Roberto picked up a clipboard from the desk and flipped through some blue paper. "Now, because you never let anyone capture the flag, we have a situation."

She folded her arms over her chest. "Have I told you how much I hate that clipboard?"

"Daily since we got here."

"At least you know."

"Here's another thing I know." He briefly looked up at her before starting on some yellow pages. "The flag is out in the study on a tray." He tucked the clipboard under his arm and glared at her. "And someone is getting it." He paused for emphasis. "From you."

She shook her head. "I don't think so."

In one motion, Roberto reclaimed the clipboard and began to read. "It says right here…"

She raised her hand to stop him. "I don't care what it says on the paper you have under your arm. You told me that the contestant who manages to capture the flag gets that date." She pointed with each word. "They didn't, so they don't."

"It says right here," he continued ignoring her, "week one, Logan goes on a date with the first contender." He flipped to the last sheet and angled it toward her. "Your signature?"

She pressed her lips together. "Yes." The words barely slipped from behind clenched teeth.

He pointed. "Then one of them gets the flag, and I suggest you start thinking about which one gets lucky."

Freddy pasted on a forced smile and entered the study with the show host. Everyone turned toward them. Logan nodded at her. Some of the contestants waved their hello.

"Ladies, if you wouldn't mind," the host said. He gestured beside him. "Logan, please join us." Logan took his place.

Freddy could feel her facial muscles begin to twitch. Holding the artificial smile on her face started to get painful. She looked at Logan. His smile seemed genuine. He might be enjoying the situation too much.

"And now the unpleasant part of the day," she heard the host continue. "One of you will be going home." The contestants groaned, some of them catching Logan's gaze and putting on an exaggerated sad face.

Oh, you bet someone's going home, Freddy thought. But she didn't know who. Panic set in. She had been so infuriated with Logan, she forgot to think about choosing one.

That had to have been his plan, she decided. No matter. She held each of the contestant's gazes one at a time. The one most googly-eyed would be toast, and right now the poet looked like the most likely candidate. *Bye-bye, blondie.*

But before she could say anything, the show host threw her a curve. "But Logan, you can save the unlucky lady."

Logan looked more interested. Freddy felt her smile slip. No one ever said anything about a save.

"If you don't agree with Freddy's choice, you can override the pick and save her."

The ladies clapped in delight.

"But," the host continued, "you only have one save and none when we get down to the final two. Plus, if you do use your save, Logan, Freddy will have to pick another lady to send home."

Groans of protest rose again. Freddy didn't like it much either. If he saved the poet, who should go?

She had no time to think about it. The show's host took her elbow and steered her toward the table with the flag. He showed her to her spot and turned to face the ladies.

"It's time for Freddy to tell us who is going home and who is going on a one-on-one date with our eligible bachelor." Then he turned to the camera across the room. "And she'll do that right after the break."

"And cut," Roberto shouted. "Three minutes, people." The key grip holding the boom mike relaxed, and the key light dimmed.

The makeup crew draped some cloth across Logan's shoulders and began dabbing at his face with sponges. "You look nice," he said as Freddy approached him.

"So do you," she replied, with her hairstylist coaxing a curl back into place and securing it with spray.

"Who's going home?" he whispered.

"Wouldn't you like to know?"

"Actually, I would."

Freddy wrinkled her nose at him. "You have a save." She jabbed him in the chest with her forefinger. "I bet that was your idea."

He held up both hands in a defensive gesture. "I found out about it the same time you did. Honest."

"I don't believe you," Freddy countered.

"I swear. I didn't know."

"Prove it."

"How?"

Freddy was about to respond when Roberto appeared and buzzed around them. "Places everyone. We're live in thirty seconds." He turned to Freddy. "When the host asks ask you who is going home, don't answer. The camera will pan the contestants for a few seconds for drama. When the camera comes back to you, tell us who will be going home." Roberto pulled her back to her spot.

The show host returned and took his place on the X taped to the floor between Freddy and Logan. One makeup artist pulled the towel from Logan's shoulders, while another scooped up the makeup-filled train case. In another second, the production crew vanished into the background. The boom mike lowered, and the key light snapped back on.

"Ten-second tape recap first and then we're live." Roberto finished with hand signals before backing away.

"Welcome back to *Eligible Bachelor.*" The show host smiled at the bachelorettes. "The first elimination challenge tested your athleticism on the paintball field. The goal was to capture the flag given to Freddy and Logan. The task seemed simple enough—six against two. So which bachelorette got the flag and the automatic date?" He motioned to a large flat-screen TV set across the room that served as a monitor. "Let's take a look."

Freddy's shoulders dropped. She was so screwed.

Everyone turned back to the show host when the video finished. He looked at Freddy. "Quite an interesting game you played."

Freddy tossed her head. "I went with my gut feeling."

"And that gut feeling was to mark everyone, including our bachelor."

She shrugged. "I got caught up in the moment."

The host gestured back to the screen. "Including this one."

Freddy's heart hammered, and she watched in stunned silence as the scene of her and Logan inside the bunker earlier in the day played out like a soap opera plot. Though the camera crew had been nowhere in sight, or at least that's what she thought, tape rolled on her time with Logan in the bunker.

Just as she suspected, the conversation was highly edited. Coupled with some creative camera shots from outside the bunker at just the right moment, the effect came out very interesting. No, she decided, "incriminating" described it better. She and Logan had been portrayed as very close that afternoon.

Fortunately, not as close as they had almost gotten thanks to Jade and her bouncing paintball. That alone would probably save her.

But Freddy would bet the proverbial ranch that her future held a very stern lecture from Roberto.

"So, Freddy, can you tell us what happened inside that bunker?" she heard the host ask.

She turned toward his voice and pasted on a smile as she saw the camera shot zoom in on her face in the monitor off to the right.

"Actually, nothing happened. Logan and I have been friends for a long time. What you saw was just us collaborating on a course of action."

"It would be interesting to find out what our viewers think." The camera homed in on the host's face. "You can post your thoughts on Facebook and Twitter or you can text your comments to the number on the bottom of the screen. Next week we'll reveal the results of what our viewing audience has to say. We'll choose the best scenario from those posted and send that lucky viewer to a night on the town in exciting New York City."

Freddy let her expression drop and quickly adjusted it. A prize for tweeting? She guessed it would be worth a whole lot of people's time to post their version of what may have happened in the bunker. She had to admit it, Roberto was making the best of what she handed him. One point for him.

"Any more thoughts on what we saw?" she heard the host ask.

She held out her hands. "What else can I say? We were in an enclosed area, hiding, and trying not to get marked." She glanced over at Logan, who just raised his eyebrows on response. She hoped the camera didn't pick it up.

"In any case," she heard the host continue, "it is time to make one bachelorette very happy when you choose her for the date for Logan and one very unhappy when you send her home."

Groans filled the air, making Freddy feel suddenly guilty. She opened her mouth to comment, but Roberto—out of camera range—made sure he caught her eye and raised the clipboard with his left hand and waggled it for emphasis.

She vowed to burn that clipboard the first chance she got. Maybe with Roberto still attached.

The host picked the flag up from the table and held it out to Freddy. "First you choose Logan's date, then we'll get to the process of sending one of our lovely bachelorettes home."

She took it hoping the camera didn't show how much her hand shook. She still had no idea who would be getting it.

She saw the cameraman with the handheld camera take a step closer to Logan. Logan's handsome face filled the TV monitor just as the host spoke.

"Logan, would you like to say something to our bachelorettes before we begin?"

He stepped forward, hands clasped. "It's been an interesting few days." He cut his gaze to Freddy before quickly returning it to the contestants. "I find this an impossible situation. Six lovely ladies and one has to go home. In the short time together here, I think I got to know all of you a little better, but I would have liked to have had more time with each of you." The camera shot moved across each of the ladies' faces, settling on Stacy, whose eyes appeared to be welling up. Logan took a handkerchief from an inside suit pocket and handed it to her.

Stacy dabbed her cheeks. "I'm going to keep this in case I'm the one sent home."

"Remember, our bachelor has a save," the host reminded.

Logan nodded his acknowledgment as the rest of the bachelorettes glared at Stacy. Slowly, he returned to his mark. Behind him, every reaction got sent coast to coast by the camera crew for the viewers to judge.

The TV drama suddenly gave Freddy an idea. Stacy would be saved for sure—saved for the rest of the ladies to take on later for trying to get a leg up on them with the snake oil tears. Being around all those five-year-olds, Stacy had probably learned how to summon up the waterworks on demand to get attention. Freddy smiled. She'd let the rest of the bachelorettes submarine the kindergarten teacher for her.

Showtime.

Taking a deep breath, Freddy took the flag and faced the bachelorettes. The cameraman shifted, moving the shot from left to right across the waiting faces. As each close-up appeared on the monitor, a wide range of emotions could be seen: hope, anger, anticipation, accompanied by some personal pleas.

Stacy had her hands together, fingertips touching her nose as if in prayer, and Jade's knuckles were white. Careelyn wrinkled her nose and waggled her fingers at the viewing audience. Emily looked over at Freddy and then locked her gaze on Logan. Lori and Madison held hands like they were BFFs.

For Freddy, that sealed Emily's fate. She wasn't getting anywhere near Logan.

Freddy took a breath. All the possibilities raced with rapid-fire speed through her mind. In dramatic fashion, she walked in front of each of the bachelorettes and made sure she held each one's gaze for agonizing seconds before moving on. After scrutinizing them one last time with a forced but barely held deadpan expression on her face, she held out the flag. "Jade, have a great time."

Jade screamed and grabbed the flag from her hand. The rest of the bachelorettes gathered around her, offering congratulations with forced smiles. Jade ran to Logan and threw her arms around his neck. His arms circled her waist while over her shoulder, he looked at Freddy.

Freddy didn't expect the wave of emotion that hit her when she saw another woman in Logan's arms. Apprehension, concern, jealousy, and fear seemed to take turns punching her in the stomach before settling inside her head and squeezing the backs of her eyes. What had she done? She had just tossed the man of her dreams into the arms of a perfect size-two runway model with great hair. Now what?

But she couldn't think much about that right now. She had to get rid of someone, if only to make herself feel better. "Oh, and by the way, Emily. Have a nice trip home."

The last thing anyone saw before the TV monitor faded to black was the horrified look on Emily's face.

Chapter Eleven

Back in his suite, Logan massaged the back of his neck, trying to shake the headache Freddy gave him. Right after she eliminated Emily, Freddy left the room.

Once filming wrapped up, he extracted himself from the bachelorettes and tried to find Freddy. He needed to talk to her, but she didn't answer when he knocked on her door. According to the schedule Roberto left on his desk, tomorrow morning after the group breakfast he had a series of fittings with representatives from Ralph Lauren in preparation for the commercials to be shown with the next airing of the series. Right afterward, he had the date with Jade, so he needed to talk to Freddy tonight.

For a while, he got caught up in watching the elimination thing torture Freddy and looked forward to finding out with whom she would set him up for the day. But the look he saw on her face when Jade hugged him really threw him off his own game, for a number of reasons.

One, for a minute, he thought Freddy might actually start crying on camera.

Two, he didn't like thinking she was hurting.

And three, he felt different around her since they started spending so much time together.

Though today's premiere episode would air in a few days during prime time around 9:00 p.m., the show taped early in the day to allow for editing. The clock on the wall said 6:00 p.m., early enough to leave a long night ahead of him. He glanced at the schedule again. Nothing pressing for the rest of the night.

He looked toward the door. Freddy couldn't hole up in her wing of the suite forever. She had to face him sooner or later. There were still five bachelorettes remaining, with four episodes left. With nothing in the contract as far as he could see forbidding him from discussing things with her, his curiosity about Freddy's thinking made him head to her side of the mansion again.

He'd like to know why she threw Emily under the bus and gave the model the date. If he had been a betting man, he would have lost his shirt on the odds in Vegas. He thought for sure Jade would have been the one packing. She'd been the most visible and the bachelorette most engaged with the activity.

At her door, an image of Freddy filled his mind almost in anticipation. He could clearly see the planes of her faces, the laughter in her eyes. He could feel the warmth of her skin, its softness. Then he thought about the kiss, so tender at first, then filled with a passion he hadn't felt in a long time.

What was happening between them? Dozens of attractive women expressed interest in him. Being single and having a great job guaranteed that. He hadn't really thought about any of the women he knew in terms of a relationship, though. At least not until now, with Freddy hell-bent on forcing one on him with this TV show.

How many hours did he spend wondering what she was going to do or what she was thinking since they were thrust into living together in this mansion? How many times did he wonder what would happen if they ditched the show and escaped somehow?

Too many to count in such a short amount of time. The situation he found himself in seemed a contradiction in terms. If he played it out to the expected end, exactly whom would he find waiting there? And if he walked away, would he possibly find something better?

Or *someone* better?

He thought back to what she said about his flaws. Weaknesses. She was right about that. He thought he had just found a big one. He balled his hand into a fist and raised it to knock on Freddy's door just as it opened.

She looked surprised to see him. "Hi."

"Hi back."

She gave him a cocked-hip pose once the surprise vanished from her face. "Done with the celebrating already?"

"For the moment."

"Why are you here?"

He offered her his hand. "Truce?"

She eyed it suspiciously. "Interesting offer. Why?"

"Can I come in?"

"I was going out."

"I'll go with you."

"You don't even know where I'm going."

"And I don't care."

Freddy sat on the imported Italian marble tile lining the main pool on the estate, her feet dangling into the cool water. Logan sat next to her, his hands braced on the tile's bullnose edging.

"Why didn't you save Emily?" she asked him.

"Why did you pick Jade?" he countered.

"You first."

He looked at her. Without makeup and her hair down, she looked every bit as beautiful as she did on the set. He liked her better this way—down to earth, natural, her hair draped past her shoulders in long, loose curls. He wondered if he ran his fingers through her hair, would it feel as silky as her skin had beneath his fingertips that day in the darkened kitchen? Only the fear of one of the production crew lurking nearby taping everything made him resist getting his answer.

"I didn't save her because you didn't want her here," he answered her.

She leaned back on her elbows, suspicion in her eyes. "That's it?"

He mimicked her pose. "That's it."

"What did you tell her?"

"I told her I enjoyed her company and wished her well."

"I mean about the fact you didn't save her."

"She didn't ask."

"I would have wanted to know why you didn't."

"If I saved her, someone else would have to go. That would mean you would have to choose someone else, and I suspected you weren't into any more drama, based on your speedy exit."

"I did kind of run out of there." She smiled, her gaze slipping past him toward the pool house.

He turned his head in the direction where she looked. "Someone there?"

"I fully expect one of the bachelorettes to come running out of the bushes any minute looking for you."

He laughed. "I'm surprised one hasn't. I think they all feel a little vulnerable after tonight."

"Except Jade." She shifted away from him, her voice distant.

"Except Jade," he agreed. "Want to tell me why she's the one you chose?"

Freddy sighed. "I wasn't very fair to her at the paintball range."

Logan shot her a knowing look. "No, you weren't."

She kicked her feet, water droplets spraying over both of them. "I've been told that I should be entertaining, not necessarily fair."

"That should make for good TV."

She kicked again. "It will." She looked at the ripples on the pool's surface. "So what time do you leave for your big date?"

"Roberto hasn't told me for sure. I suppose I'll find a note or a script or something once I get back to the suite."

Freddy nodded. "I'm sure you'll have a nice time."

"Where would you go on a first date?"

As soon as the words left his mouth, his chest tightened. What had possessed him? It was bad enough he had to traipse around town with a woman he hardly knew with cameras in his face—it was worse yet to ask Freddy where to take her.

He saw her face register shock with his question, but only for a moment before she appeared to regain her composure. "It isn't me going."

"But what if it was," he pressed.

"Are you asking me for a date?"

Logan forced himself not to show the curiosity her question had stirred in him. "I don't think anything like that is on Roberto's clipboard."

She rolled her eyes. "One of these days, I'm going to put that clipboard where Roberto will never find it."

"Then?"

She bit down on her lip in an unsuccessful attempt to hide her smile. "Then we'll see what happens."

"So you admit then, you'd like to go on a date with me."

"I admit that as a teenager, I wanted to go on lots of dates with you." Her smile broke free. "But that was before I held myself to a much higher standard."

"A higher standard?" The words came out like a laugh.

She straightened and swiveled her head toward him. "Definitely. You couldn't handle me on the football field. How do you think you can handle me on the dating field?"

Before he could stop himself, he put his hand on her shoulder. He could feel the delicate curve of her collarbone and caressed it with his thumb.

"What are you doing?" she asked him.

What was he doing? He had no idea. Reluctantly, he let her go. "That game was a fluke. No one else ever stopped me from scoring again."

"On the football field or"—she hesitated—"or on the dating field," she continued with a smile.

"I probably shouldn't be talking to you about this," he said.

"Maybe not," she agreed.

He forced himself not to mention the fiery red color creeping across her cheeks, taking his curiosity higher. "You can tell me it's none of my business or you can push me into the pool, but why didn't you ever let me know that you were interested in me?"

"I sent signals."

He snickered. "You did not."

"I most certainly did."

"Then I never got them."

"Typical jock not to notice." She sounded annoyed. "You were too busy trying to score with the head cheerleader most of the time."

"How did you know? We weren't in the same school."

"Everyone knew. Sophomore year, I met a nice guy at the library. Dinner and a movie date. A nice date. We sat in the same row as you and blondie rah-rah at the movie theater, and you never even acknowledged me."

"I don't remember seeing you."

"You never saw the movie either. Malibu Barbie was all over you."

"That was a whole lot of years ago. How am I supposed to remember that?"

"I bet you remember her."

His crooked smile broke. "She *was* all over me."

She pushed him playfully. "Like white on rice."

"Jealous?"

"No!" she dragged out the word. "She was all over everybody she dated."

"Unlike you and your dates."

She stopped smiling and looked down at the water. "That guy. The library guy. He was the only date I had the whole year." She looked at him. "And not even a good night kiss. Not a real one anyway, and I know you know what I mean."

He felt really foolish. "Why no more dates?"

"I guess the word got out."

"What word?"

"That I was the proverbial Goody Two-shoes. You know how it was back then. The testosterone scorecard ruled."

"Part of the rites of passage, however unfair it seems now."

"I guess," she acknowledged. "But no one had an interest in seeing me after that, and after a while, I lost interest in dating."

"Didn't you feel like you were missing out on the whole high school experience?"

She shook her head no, but he could tell from her expression that it wasn't the truth. "I couldn't miss what I didn't know. I got busy with clubs and things." She began talking faster. "And it's not like I didn't talk to guys the whole time. I did. So it's not like I became an actual hermit or anything." She raised a finger as if in warning. "And I do fine now, so don't read anything into it, okay?"

He scooted next to her and looped his arm around her waist. "For what it's worth, we all want the Goody Two-shoes after we grow up."

She snickered. "Thanks to jocks like you, there aren't many of us left these days."

"Which should make you more in demand."

"That's comforting."

"So are you?"

Her head snapped up. "Am I what?"

"In demand these days?"

She laughed. "Wouldn't you like to know."

"Yes. I would."

"As I said, I do okay."

He glanced sideways at her. She seemed lost in thought. "What about the good night kisses? I bet they are real now."

"Depends on the situation."

Logan's arm surrounded her again. "What about this situation?"

He thought she was about to ask him to move his hand or make some excuse to leave, but she did neither. Instead, she leaned over and put her hand on top of his before kissing him on the cheek. "Between friends like us, kisses are innocent."

As if on instinct, he turned to her, his face only an inch from hers, and his heart seemed to stop. Kissing her the way he wanted to at this moment would never be innocent.

Chapter Twelve

A wave of panic rushed through Freddy's stomach as she stared at Logan's lips. Her hand still rested on his, and she started to remove it, but he covered it.

"Maybe we should head back inside," she suggested. But she failed to move away.

"Maybe we should."

Logan didn't move either. Their gazes locked. Logan raised his hand and cradled her face. Slowly, he moved closer and touched his lips to hers. It only lasted a second, but for Freddy, it felt like a lifetime.

"What are you doing?" Her voice was barely a whisper.

"Kissing you good night."

The straightforward admission made her heart nearly stop beating. Then he did it again.

This time, the restraint he'd showed during the first kiss disappeared, replaced by a sense of passion and desire, as though she had given him permission. And maybe she had by not pulling away.

She shuddered and closed her eyes, allowing the sensation of his lips on hers to overwhelm her. How many times had she thought about how it would feel if Logan kissed her? How many times had she dreamed it would be like this?

There was no way she would pull away from him. Not after so many years of waiting. Instead, impulse overruled common sense, and she clutched his T-shirt, holding him tight against her.

Logan angled himself toward her, his powerful arms surrounding her as he kissed her ear, her cheek, her chin. Like two teenagers making out at the backyard pool, they hugged and kissed as though they only had minutes before their parents would come home and catch them.

Catch them.

Not their parents.

Cameras.

With telephoto lenses.

"No, no, no, this is bad." She barely got the words out with the rush of adrenaline that pumped through her body. "We're not alone. We're never alone here." Logan raised his head and met her gaze. The desire in his eyes made her want to go back to kissing him.

"I'm sorry. You're right. I lost my head."

"We'll lose more than that if someone sees us." She pushed against his chest and flew up to standing.

She ran toward the pool house like she had been shot from a canon. Glancing back, she waved for him to follow her. She saw his forehead wrinkle in confusion, but he did as asked.

Her hand shook as she turned the doorknob of the changing room. Breathing a sigh of relief that it hadn't been locked, she pushed it open. Once they were safely inside, Logan put his hand on her shoulder, and she turned toward his touch.

"I should have never taken such liberty out there. I just wanted..."

Freddy waved him off. "It's okay. I don't know for sure if there are any security cameras or otherwise in the pool area, but I'm pretty sure there are none in here."

His fingers flexed on her shoulder and the muscles of his face relaxed as he took in a breath. "So you're saying you're fine with—" He stopped and waggled his eyebrows up and down.

"You bet I am!" she said, reaching up and forking her fingers in his hair the way she dreamed she would since she decided he was the one. Ignoring his confused look, she stretched onto her tiptoes, pulled his face down to hers, and kissed him the way she'd never kissed any other man in her life. When he deepened the kiss, she sighed. This is how she thought it would feel in his arms. Maybe she could make up for all that lost time. She moved her hand to his chest, her fingertips at the hollow of his neck.

Logan jerked, and for a split second, she wondered if she had done the right thing. "Did you hear something?" he asked, angling his ear toward the door.

The only thing she heard had been the blood pounding in her ears. "No."

Logan spun on his heels, grabbed her hand, and walked to a window on the right side of the pool house. He pressed himself against the wall and urged her to do the same. Then he put a finger to his lips, suggesting she stay quiet.

That's when she heard what he had. Voices. Two of them.

"Did you see which way they went?"

"I think it was this way!"

Freddy held her breath.

"What about the pool house?"

Logan crouched down and eased his way over to the door as the voices got closer. Reaching out, he slowly turned the dead bolt lock almost at the same time someone from the outside tried to turn the doorknob.

"It's locked." The knob rattled. "I don't have a key."

"So if it's locked, then no one went inside, doofus." The second voice returned. "Look around. I'm sure I saw them go this way."

As the voices trailed off, Logan crept to the window and rose up until his eyes were level with the bottom sill. She glanced at him; he didn't seem to share her concern. In fact, he was having a hard time containing his laughter from the way his body was shaking.

"What's so funny?" she whispered.

"You should see those two. They are beating the bushes looking for us."

"What if they go back to the house for the key?"

"We're not locked in, Freddy. They are locked out. Once they leave, we can make a break for it."

She shot him a venomous look. "I know that."

Logan stood, his face full in the window now. "They're gone." He turned to her.

"Then we should probably not waste any time getting out of here."

"Yeah, think about how they would edit this. The eligible bachelor and his yenta sneaking around in the dark trying to find a place to get a little—"

She cut him off with what sounded like snarl. "Get a little what?"

"Fresh air. Get your mind out of the gutter."

She glared at him before smiling. "I knew that. Quit talking, and let's move. You said it. Who knows what an imaginative editor might be able to put together for the show."

Logan shook his head. "I don't think the show would have needed an editor." He puckered his lips and made a kissing sound. "Remember?"

All too well, she thought. "I got caught up in the romance of the show."

"There is no romance in the show."

"Of course there is. There's a beautiful mansion and six weeks of luxury with a promise of the date of a lifetime at the end. It's a perfect setting."

"But it isn't real."

"Neither was the kiss." How did she manage *that* lie?

"It felt real to me."

"Would you have kissed me under other, more normal circumstances? Say if we were in the parking lot outside your office or in my mom's backyard?"

"That's not a fair question, Freddy."

"It's more than fair, so answer it." He hesitated, giving her the answer she didn't want. "Never mind. We should never have done this."

He was beside her in a second and took her hand. "Do you really mean that?"

"Yes. We've known each other for a long time. Since we were kids. If you were going to kiss me for real, it would have happened already. It didn't." She shrugged her hand free. "Now, let's go. We have a show to finish."

Chapter Thirteen

The next morning, Logan didn't slow his pace until he hit the three-mile mark on his daily run. He threw his head back and sucked in the crisp morning air before bending over and putting his hands on his knees to stretch his back.

He stared down at the dirt path. Despite Freddy's dismissal of what happened last night, something had changed between them. True, they had done a lot together since they'd met as kids. Freddy seemed interested in the same things he liked in grade school, like football. He smiled. She had a mean chop block.

Later, during the high school years, they had done homework and research projects together, albeit for different schools. He guessed he couldn't have passed physics without her. Then they stayed in touch during college via the usual social networking sites and connected again afterward. She helped him more times than he could count with gifts for girlfriends for birthdays and holidays, and they always remembered each other for the same reasons. They were friends, buds, someone he turned to when he needed someone to talk to.

But then they began spending twenty-four hours in the same house together and something happened. He discovered some feelings he had weren't strictly friendly.

He needed to figure out why now. Could it be the confines of the mansion? The thrill of the chase associated with the show? Or could it be something deeper?

Still debating, he turned and headed back to the house, pounding the dirt path until sweat stung his eyes. After a time, he slowed his steps and squinted against the sun at the manor ahead as Lori and Stacy jogged up next to him.

"Getting in shape for the big date?" Lori asked him.

"And I see you are keeping up with your military PE," Logan countered.

Lori smiled. "Thanks for noticing."

He turned to Stacy. "Is she training you?" he quipped.

She shook her head. "Just want to be sure the five-year-olds don't outrun me when I get back."

Over Stacy's shoulder, he could see Roberto waving at him from the edge of the gardens. He pointed. "I think that's my cue, ladies." Both women looked back at the mansion in response. "I bet Roberto would rival your basic training drill sergeant," he said to Lori.

She laughed. "Better not keep him waiting then." She smiled. "Although, I wouldn't mind if you kept Jade waiting all day and missed the date entirely."

"I'll second that," Stacy cut in.

"Now you wouldn't want me to miss our dates, would you?" Logan asked. Both ladies shook their heads. "So I'll go this way," he pointed to the mansion, "and I'll let you two continue your workout." He hitched his thumb over his shoulder. "If you follow the path, up about two miles is some county parkland with a more level trail."

"Thanks," they called out in unison as they ran by him.

He shook his head and stabbed his fingers into his hair, brushing the damp locks away from his face. He blew out a long breath of air as a frazzled Roberto approached.

"I need to talk to you," Roberto insisted.

"Sure, right after I shower."

"No, now. It's too serious for that."

Freddy sat at the mile-long cherrywood table set up for production conferences in the basement of the mansion. Back straight, shoulders square, she rested her folded hands on the highly polished surface and waited. This would not be good. She could feel it. She looked up when Roberto and Logan entered.

Logan pulled out a chair and slid into it, as did Roberto. "What's up?" He looked from Freddy to Roberto to Freddy. "Are we going over logistics of the date?"

He grabbed the hem of his T-shirt and wiped his face with it, exposing his bare stomach with its defined abs. Freddy sucked in a deep breath with the sight.

She saw Logan grin when he noticed. "I just ran three miles or so this morning, and Roberto waylaid me before I could get in the shower."

"Enough chitchat," Roberto said, his voice snappish. "What have you two been doing since you got here?"

"Stuff," Logan shrugged and glanced at Freddy. "Why?"

She looked at him, wariness doing laps around her brain, hitting every sensory receptor she owned. Maybe the production crew caught them on film in the pool house somehow. She glanced at Roberto. His forehead bore more creases than the wrinkled linen jacket he wore, and they deepened with each passing moment. The warning voice inside her head sounded like the robot from *Lost in Space*, "Warning, Frederika McAllister. Warning. Warning."

Roberto did not say another word. He reached behind him and pressed the play button on the control panel hooked up to the flat-screen TV sitting on the credenza. The screen brightened, and Freddy felt sick. Someone had filmed her and Logan in the mansion's kitchen during the blackout. No audio accompanied the scene, obviously shot with a night-vision lens.

A sickening awareness took hold as she watched the scene unfold. "No, no, that is not what you think!" She glared at Logan. "Tell him!"

The scene continued. As though an arctic blast froze her to the chair, she watched Logan, outlined in the green of the infrared light, lean in to nearly kiss her. Fortunately, the angle was bad. You couldn't really tell what happened. Logan could have been doing anything, from getting something from the counter behind her to whispering in her ear. She remembered her hands on his shoulders and his hands on her hips, but the cameraman had shifted to a close-up and showed the embrace. With some editing and clever narrative, the kissing seed could be planted in the mind of the viewing audience. Still, it could be worse.

Logan tunneled his fingers in his hair and let out a long breath of air. "It looks kind of sexy, doesn't it?"

Openmouthed, Freddy looked at him and blinked twice. "Sexy?" she asked through clenched teeth.

Roberto ignored her. "Keep watching."

Then it got worse. The picture shook, as if the camera had changed hands, and then the close-up she'd never wanted came into focus on the screen. Her chin rested on Logan's shoulder and she appeared to be enjoying the feel of his cheek next to her neck. While he hadn't kissed her that day, it seemed they were getting mighty close to it.

Suddenly, the camera shot burned to white when the lights came back on inside the mansion when the electricity was restored.

Roberto didn't waste a second. "I don't know what was going on, and I don't care." He pointed at Freddy. "I'll sue you both for fraud if I have to, but this show is going on, as scheduled and according to script. The teasers go on the network this week during prime time, and the commercials for the series have been shot. We're talking millions of dollars here in revenue for the network and the producers. Are you prepared to reimburse everyone if the show doesn't air?"

"No," she answered in a small voice. She saw Logan slump back in his seat in surrender.

Roberto held her gaze. "Need I remind you that you are the one who sent in Mr. Gabriel's photo?"

"No."

"Or that the magazine has put a lot of time and effort into this?"

"No."

"And the network has already put out a lot of money." He reached for his clipboard.

"I know, I know. The contract." Fortunately for Roberto, he withdrew his hand. If he had shaken that clipboard in her face one more time, she was sure she would have exploded. She had some serious proverbial tap dancing to do until she could figure a way out.

"So then, what was going on in the kitchen that night?" Roberto gestured to Logan. "His male hormones I can understand, but you." He pointed to Freddy. "You started this, and we expect you to finish it."

She certainly did start it. She took a mighty sexy picture of Logan and sent it in to the magazine. Just her luck to win something besides the lottery. Now for both their sakes, she had to see this little adventure she had gotten them into through to the bitter end. The *very* bitter end.

"I can explain the video."

Roberto leaned forward and rested his arms on the table. "Please. By all means do."

Logan leaned forward. "Freddy..."

She cut him off before he could finish. "Logan, it's all on me. I got you into this. I'll help you get through it." She closed her eyes for a brief second and took in a small, calming breath she hoped no one noticed. "Nothing happened in the kitchen, and nothing ever would have. Logan and I are like family. It was all strictly innocent. He's like my brother."

"Are you sure?"

"Totally." The word came out in a rush of air.

Roberto turned to Logan. "Is that true?"

He shrugged. "She's driving."

"Look," Freddy said quickly, "I've never been a quitter, and I'm not going to start now." She caught Logan's gaze. "Besides, you know your firm is totally on board. With all the publicity this show brings and all the attention your firm will get, appearing on *Eligible Bachelor* could give you a great career boost."

"I'm not worried about my career, Freddy," Logan countered.

"You should be," Roberto cut in. "Your ad agency is going to play a key role in one of your dates."

Freddy snapped her head around to look at Roberto. "What?"

"We have arranged with the managing partner at Logan's firm to use the winning bachelorette in the ad campaign you were working on."

Logan cut him off with a dismissive wave. "Ad campaigns can be tricky. Clients don't like experiments."

"We'll be using a version of your Bio-Shoe ads, but jazz it up a little with our contacts. Your boss seemed very excited about the new concept."

Logan blew out a long breath. "Now I am worried about my career. That is an important account." The skeptical look on

Logan's face revealed more than the dubious tone of his voice. "I've been courting that account for months. A bad presentation could send the client to another firm." He rose and began to pace. "I mean, it's more than a PowerPoint presentation. You need the right setting, the right mood, an experienced model and production crew, and my concept includes the Arizona desert."

"Relax," Roberto assured. "We'll be taking care of everything."

Freddy's blood kicked into a slow, angry simmer as she listened to the details. Heck, Logan hadn't even gone on the first date yet, and already there were plans to fly across the country and use his dream date to solidify his marketing career. She thought her veins would burst as the temperature of her blood probably reached that of the Arizona desert in August.

She opened her mouth to say something, but nothing came out. No words. No protests. No sounds. Nothing. She looked at Logan. He looked surprised. She sure was.

Roberto looked from Logan to Freddy. "Unless there is actually something going on between the two of you that would prevent the show from continuing."

Freddy cut her eyes to Logan. Was there something between them? She knew she felt more than just friendship, but then again, she always had. Even when they were kids.

But that might be all it ever was and ever would be—the adolescent crush of a girl who never got any closer to the sports jock than helping him with his science homework or history report. Then he grew up and moved on. Maybe now she should also.

She wouldn't take this opportunity from him—the chance to grab the brass ring in the marketing world and see where it would take him. He deserved that. She would make sure he had it.

"There is no reason Logan can't finish this show. There's nothing going on between us," she said, looking at her hands in her lap.

"Then I don't have to worry about the video."

"Not in the least," Freddy said quickly. She met Logan's gaze with her own, hoping he couldn't read how she really felt. "There never was anything besides friendship between us and never will be."

Logan returned her gaze with a look that gutted her in place. "We're just friends."

Freddy willed her cheeks not to color and the emotional turmoil welling up inside her not to reach her eyes. "I'm sure the ad shoot will be great."

"Then until this show is over, you will be somewhere I can keep an eye on you. There is too much invested for anything to go wrong now." He sat back. "Do we all understand each other?"

Gazes on each other, both Freddy and Logan nodded

Roberto slapped his hands together before looking at his watch. "Good. Then, Logan, I suggest you get ready. You leave with Jade for your date in one hour." Without waiting for either one to reply, he stood and left the room.

Chapter Fourteen

"So," Logan said, his smile humorless. "That went well."

Freddy reached out and smacked him as hard as she could on his upper arm. He covered the area she hit with his hand. "Ow. What was that for?"

"The video clip we just saw. All your doing."

"I don't remember being alone in it." He lifted one corner of his mouth, his gaze penetrating her. "And I don't remember anyone saying no to all my suggestions."

Her stomach seemed to melt into a puddle in the center of her body from the long look he gave her. "It was our first day here. We were just getting settled and adjusted to the place."

"I suppose."

"No suppose. Fact. We got whisked away without time to think about anything, driven to this incredible place, and told it was ours for the next few weeks. While we still reeled from that, Roberto pulled out his clipboard and speed-talked a list of things we had to do."

"Then the lights went out."

"And came back on."

He sat back and arched an arm across the back of the chair, easily drawing her attention to the way the fabric of his shirt pulled across his chest. "Imagine what might have happened if they hadn't come back on so soon."

A PowerPoint presentation of her own with all the possibilities began playing in her head. If he wanted to distract her from the day ahead of her, mission accomplished. But only for a moment. The suggestion changed nothing, and neither would her answer to it.

"That doesn't matter now." He looked disappointed. "But now that we have had time to get used to this place and what's expected of us, you know what that means now, don't you?"

He shook his head.

"We're outnumbered by people who will make sure we stick to the rules and see this show to the end."

He unwound his arm from the backrest and leaned toward her. "And what do you think that end might be?"

She put a forefinger on his chest and symbolically held him back. "However it is they want it to end. I don't need any more complications."

He grabbed her hand and flattened it against his chest. "Then we're even, because neither do I."

She could feel his heart beating rapidly against his rib cage and wondered briefly if the beat steadily rose because of excitement or anger. "Maybe we should talk about strategy."

"No can do. I have a date in about an hour, remember?" He held her gaze with his.

Though the pressure of his grasp lightened, she didn't remove her hand, but let her palm absorb the warmth she found there. "And I suppose I should get to know the also-rans you leave behind. I have to let another one go home soon." She started to ease away, but he tightened his grip. She looked from his hand to his eyes. "There's too much invested for something to go wrong now." She tugged her hand free of his and rose. "That's what Roberto said, remember?"

She'd found the bright pink pool float in the pool house, the kind only sold in high-end pool shops and mail-order houses. Ads said the float was virtually unsinkable, and she decided she'd just proved the claim true. She'd been floating on it in the deep end of the huge pool for about two hours. It hadn't dipped even an inch below the water when she turned over, which was a good thing, considering she planned to stay in the sun until her brain reached "bake" temperature and forced her to forget about Logan and his date. Another hour should do it, she decided, adjusting her sunglasses.

Distinctly female voices made her glance toward the sound. Great. The preppie and the beauty queen. Two reminders that her body was in no shape to handle the type of bathing suit they had on. The material from her conservative one-piece could probably make both of theirs.

She closed her eyes and stayed perfectly still, hoping they would think she was asleep. Her ruse apparently did not work because she heard two splashes and felt the float rock in the small wave that was made.

A hand grabbed on to the edge of the float near her head. Madison's voice followed. "You're turning as pink as this raft."

Freddy opened her eyes enough to see Madison looked great even when wet. "I guess the sunblock isn't as waterproof as it claims," she replied. She heard splashing to her right and turned her head in time to see Careelyn surface.

Careelyn bobbed in the water and brushed her hair away from her face with one hand. Freddy noticed that not only did her mascara not move, but neither did the eyeliner that rimmed her blue eyes. She made a mental note to ask for some waterproof mascara the next time she saw one of the makeup artists.

"Why don't we all sit in the cabana and get to know each other?" Careelyn suggested, grabbing on to the float and helping Madison propel it to the pool's edge.

Freddy smiled. "If we must." They were slick, these two. There would be no escaping them. She glanced around as much as she could and saw no camera crew in sight. Production was probably following Logan and Jade around. Maybe she could find out something she could use to send these two packing one by one.

Madison and Careelyn maneuvered her to the shallow end of the pool where she easily hopped off the float and out of the water with the bachelorettes right on her heels. With one woman on each side of her, she had no recourse but to walk with them to the shady area under the triangular sunshade set above the patio. Once there, she picked up a thick green towel and dried off. Then after raking her hair back with one hand, she eased herself into one of four chaises.

While the two women arranged chairs in front of her like a wall, she noticed that her skin looked well past pink and on its way to bright red. It was so going to hurt later. She looked up and saw Madison and Careelyn smiling at her. She felt like prey let loose at a game preserve. Okay then, if that's how they wanted to play it, game on.

"And how are you enjoying this little adventure so far?" Freddy asked, adjusting her backrest and feeling the canvas scrape against her sunburned back. Apparently, she would be uncomfortable in more ways than one during this little chat. "Is it all you thought it would be?"

"Not at all," Madison replied. "I don't think any of us knew you were going to be here with us."

At least Roberto had surprised everyone. "How do you like the mansion?" Freddy asked.

"It's beautiful and…"

Careelyn threw up her hand. "Let's stop the chitchat, shall we, and cut right to the real reason we came out here. Who's going home next, and it better not be me."

Points to Careelyn for directness, Freddy thought. "Well, I haven't decided yet." She kept her tone even and calm, but inside her annoyance simmered.

"What will it take to convince you not to send one of us home?"

"I'm not into making alliances. I think you need to be on *Survivor* for that."

"Cute." Careelyn's voice oozed sarcasm. "For this you have to be the last one standing, too." Freddy noticed that Careelyn had all but lost her southern accent. "Where did you say you were from?"

"The Southeast," she responded, falling back into a drawl. "Why?"

Southeast Brooklyn, maybe. "No reason. Just wondering," Freddy smiled and turned to Madison. "What about you?"

"Boston. But not the city proper, more like a suburb." Her accent was real. "Why? Does it matter where we're from? Because I could move. I just graduated from college and haven't landed a job yet. That's why I sent in the application for the show."

"To get a job?" Freddy asked.

"Not exactly. But the experience will be good for me, don't you think?"

I think both of you are going home, one right after the other, Freddy thought, maintaining an even, forced smile. She moved forward on the chaise, and the backs of her thighs screamed with pain when she slid across the rough canvas cushion. She glanced at her arms, a bright red contrast to the white wicker chaise. Her stomach began to reel but she couldn't decide if it was reacting to the sunburn or the company.

"I think I need to find some cream," she announced, rising. "I may have stayed a tiny bit too long in the sun." Madison and Careelyn said nothing, only watched her step over the ottoman next to her. "I'll see you both tonight."

"Better stay hydrated," Madison called out as Freddy left. "It would be a shame if you couldn't come to elimination."

"No, it wouldn't," Careelyn said, shushing her. "Maybe then no one would be sent home for at least another day."

Freddy turned and smiled. "I'll be there," she promised. "And someone *will* be leaving."

She walked out from the shade, and the sun hit her shoulders, making her wince. As she dashed from shady spot to shady spot on her way into the mansion, she decided she finally knew what it must feel like to be barbecued. The headache hit her when she got as far as the sliding door. A feeling of nausea followed.

In trying to forget Logan's date with Jade for a time, she'd doomed herself to about a day or two of pain and a stint as a lovely shade of red. The last time she did something this stupid was the time she went to the Jersey Shore on a class trip in high school. She'd baked herself over a guy then, too—the lifeguard on duty. She spent the next day in bed and a few more days peeling flaking skin all over the school.

Gingerly, she made her way through the mansion, wincing with every step she took. As she passed one of the powder rooms on the first floor, she reached out and eased the door open. Slowly, she raised her gaze to the mirror. She looked like Lobster Girl. It was going to be a very long and very painful night.

Chapter Fifteen

Logan tapped on the door leading to Freddy's suite and pushed it open. "You in here?"

"Yes, but stay out."

He ignored her. "You're mad at me for going on the date, aren't you?"

"I am not."

"Then what's the problem?" He stepped inside the room and saw the problem immediately.

Still wearing her bathing suit, Freddy lay on the bed, eyes closed, on top of the thousand-thread-count sheets. The stark contrast of red skin against the white sheets looked painful to him. He walked over and sat on the edge of the bed. "What on earth did you do?"

"Ouch, ouch, ouch," Freddy groaned as the mattress shifted with Logan's weight. Even the luxury sheets didn't stop the painful abrasion against her sensitive skin. She opened one eye. "Stop moving."

"You look like…"

She cut him off. "Don't say it."

He finished anyway. "Like you've been boiled in oil."

"I think that would have been less painful." She opened both eyes. "I floated in the pool a little too long."

"How long?"

"All afternoon."

He shook his head. "You never heard of sunscreen?"

"Yes."

"It doesn't do any good unless you put it on."

"Ha-ha." The pause between words announced her annoyance.

He shifted, and she groaned again. "Every time you move, you make every part of me touching something hurt, so stop." He got up, and she gave him as much of a surly look as her sunburned face would allow.

He stood over her, hands on hips, a real look of concern on his face. "You do look awful."

"Thanks for the critique." She began to struggle to a sitting position. He extended his hand. She took it and eased herself to the edge of the bed, grimacing all the way.

"You really should put something on that sunburn." He started to sit down, but stopped. "Can I?" He gestured to a spot next to her.

"Only if you are as stealthy as possible." She shut her eyes tight and waited.

Gingerly, he lowered himself down. "What on earth were you thinking?"

She opened her eyes and looked his way. "I was thinking I didn't want the bachelorettes to grill me all afternoon while they waited for you to come back from your date with Jade, and I didn't want to lock myself up here for the whole day. So I thought if I floated in the middle of the pool, they'd leave me alone."

"And I guess they did."

"Sounded like a better idea than it actually turned out to be."

Logan leaned back. "Let me see what you did to yourself." He made a disapproving tsk-tsking sound as he checked her back and arms. "I think you're going to blister."

Freddy sighed. "Red and bubbly. That should make for good TV. The viewers will love that."

"You can't go to the elimination tonight," Logan said.

"Why not?"

"How are you supposed to get into a dress when ninety percent of you can't stand the feel of anything?"

"You heard Clipboard Man. There is nothing either of us can do but finish this stupid game."

"Show, not game."

"Whatever."

"That's not important now." His palm hovered over her back. He could feel heat emanating from her skin. "You're going to be really uncomfortable for a few days unless we do something about this right now." As carefully as possible he rose, still managing to jostle the bed enough to have Freddy wince. "I'm going to call Roberto so you can get to a doctor."

Freddy jumped to her feet, ignoring how uncomfortable the action made her. "Don't you dare. I'll be fine."

"You won't be fine. Your skin is going to feel tighter as the day goes on." He gently lifted her arm. "Plus, I'm pretty sure you're going to be one big blister by morning."

"Maybe not."

"Trust me, Freddy. I come from a family of sun worshippers. And with football practice in the summer, any part of me not covered by equipment was not spared the effects of hours in the sun. Mom knew just what to do, and because of it, so do I." He walked to the door. "Stay put. I'll be right back."

She shot him an impudent look. "I can't even get out of my bathing suit without help. Where am I going?"

For a long moment, he stared at her before running his gaze down her length and back up to her eyes. "Good point," he said, raising his right hand. "So if you need a volunteer for that, I'm your man."

In the kitchen, Logan ripped open the refrigerator door and found the milk. After setting it on the counter, he foraged through the mass of kitchen cabinets until he found a large stainless steel pot.

Milk and cool water. His mother's homemade remedy for sunburn. For once, he was happy he'd spent all those summers on the football field in the sun. He watched the water and milk mix into a white opaque solution.

A smile curled his mouth, his mind drifting back to the last time he found himself in the kitchen. With Freddy. On this very counter.

That's the night it began—the thought maybe she could be more than just a friend. The feeling crept up on him like a patient stalker at first, but now, thinking back, he couldn't help but wonder how long it had been building. Days? Months? Years?

He'd always looked forward to seeing her at their regularly scheduled gatherings with friends, and he made sure she stayed near him. He liked her, sure, but he had liked a lot of women over the years. He'd grown particularly fond of a few of them. Fond enough to date one or two, for more than a few months even.

But he ended each relationship when he felt the walls closing in on him. Talk of something more permanent, like structure and limits and kids, did it for him every time. That's when he pulled back—when someone tried to pull him into the predictable holding pattern of life as part of a couple. He didn't like being that conventional; he liked the surprises life could hand a person.

Like the one he was having now. None of the women he'd dated would have done something as spontaneous as entering his picture in a contest or leaving a familiar routine to do reality TV. Now, however, because of just that, he had the strange notion that he'd had someone pretty darn amazing under his nose all along and he'd never noticed her.

Okay, so maybe he had been a bit annoyed when the escapade started, but not now. Now he thought he would like to see what could develop because of it. He wanted more time with Freddy. More time to find out what she might do. More time to hear her laugh.

He shook his head. What was wrong with him anyway? Why hadn't he felt this way before? Could it be real or just the excitement of the adventure?

Falling for her, if that's what was happening, defied logic. They'd been friends for years, friends when they were kids, and friends now. If something were going to happen, it would have happened a long time ago. Even she had said that.

So why couldn't he help but think something might be happening now?

As he reached over and turned the faucet off, he pictured the liquid running down Freddy's reddened back in creamy droplets. In his mind, he drizzled more of the milk water over her shoulders and watched as the drops reached her waist. He felt his breath catch, and it shook him back to reality.

He stabbed his fingers through his hair. This was crazy, him thinking of her like that. Maybe some things were better left unchanged.

Freddy managed to get to the chair in the dressing room. She could almost feel her skin tighten against her muscles by the minute, the sunburn sucking every bit of moisture left in her body. Baking in the sun in the middle of the pool to avoid the rest of the bachelorettes had been a terrible idea, one she wouldn't soon forget. She sat on the edge of the chair in the dressing room and contemplated her next move.

Elimination was only a few hours away. She needed to find a dress that wouldn't feel like sandpaper running across her baked back. She started to get up but was immediately told to sit back down by the painful message sent to her brain via her burnt thighs. She eased herself back down onto the caned seat and decided she should just sit there until her skin turned back to its normal color. How long could that possibly take? A few weeks at the most?

"I have some aspirin and my mom's surefire home remedy for you." Logan came in holding the large pasta pot—with both hands— a bottle of aspirin, and a box of baking soda tucked under his arm.

Freddy watched him set the pot and the baking soda down before holding out the aspirin bottle to her. She scanned the label, checking the brand, before taking two tablets without water. At this point, she wanted to dull the pain that ran from the widow's peak of her head to the tips of her toes as fast as possible.

"Thanks." She watched him pick up the pot and the baking soda and walk into the bathroom.

"Follow me," he called back to her.

She heard water running. "Why?"

"I'm going to make you feel a whole lot better."

Every part of her body that was bright red ached as she struggled to a standing position. "This better be good."

"I promise, it will be."

She stopped at the doorway. Logan knelt next to the large jetted bathtub filling with water and emptied the baking soda box into it. The pasta pot sat on the floor next to his knees. "I'm not getting into that. If I do, I'll never get out."

He held out his hand. "It's a no-fail treatment for what ails you right now, trust me."

Though skeptical, she reached toward him. She barely felt his touch when he took her hand and urged her forward. She looked at the marble tub and sighed, ignoring the way her bathing suit straps cut into her sunburned shoulders when she did. "At least it will feel good against my back."

He helped her get settled and then turned the jets on to the lowest setting. She closed her eyes and leaned against the back of the white marble, feeling the cool water splash against her skin. For the first time in a few hours, she didn't feel someone could cook hot dogs on her.

Her eyes flew open when she heard more splashing and felt water trickle across her shoulders and down her arms. Logan was cupping his hands in the water and trailing it over her skin.

"That feels wonderful," she whispered, relishing how the cool liquid doused the fire on her skin. She could almost hear her over-worked nerve endings sigh.

"The baking soda I put in here helps cool the skin. When we're done, we will let it dry to a powder instead of toweling it off, to help with retaining moisture."

"I can't do that. I can't look like I've been rolled in flour at elimination tonight."

"I thought you might say that, so remedy number two is in the pasta pot."

"What is it?"

"Milk."

She made a face. "The last thing I feel like drinking is milk."

"It's not to drink. It's to wear. Sit up."

She furrowed her brow even though it hurt to do so.

Logan caught the doubt that showed on her face. "C'mon. Sit. You're going to feel a whole lot better in a minute." He reached into the water and put his hand on the small of her back, urging her up.

She sucked in a small breath when he touched her. Even though cool water surrounded her, his hand felt hotter than her sunburn did. The heat enhanced his earthy, masculine scent, blending it with the sterile scent of the baking soda and cloaking her with a pleasant aroma. So far, she liked his remedy. It almost made her forget the pain.

"This may be cold," he said, his other hand splashing in the pasta pot next to him. "But it will be worth it, I promise."

"You're promising me an awful lot today," she quipped.

"Trust me."

She looked at him. "I do."

The water that snaked down her spine when he drizzled it over her back ran right into the tingle of anticipation that raced up it. She had to admit, both felt really good. "Maybe you do know what you're doing."

"I have to. I can't do this show without you."

Her stomach sank with the reminder. "So you're only doing this just to make sure I do what I'm supposed to do in the contract?" The question hung in the air, thickening it with tension.

"Is that what you think?"

Her defenses rose. "It's what you said."

"Wrong choice of words on my part, I suppose." He moved his hand from her back. "Lean forward."

She raised her knees and rested her cheek on her kneecaps, her hands circling her legs. She closed her eyes as cool water began running down her heated back. "You can do this all night." Her voice came out in a sigh. "It feels great."

"And it's about to get better."

The sunburn sting actually seemed to subside. "Can't possibly."

The splashing stopped. "It may be a bit of a shock, but try not to move."

"What are you going to do, get in here with me?"

"Wouldn't that be something for the editors?"

Even as a smile pulled the tender red skin on her face tighter, she laughed. Then suddenly something colder than the water in which she soaked hit her square in the back. On contact, she arched her back and inhaled sharply.

"Told you it might be a shock," Logan said.

He began gently patting her back, and she realized he'd put a cloth over it. "What did you put on me?"

"Milk on a hand towel." He removed the towel and soaked it again. "Ready for another round?"

"I have to admit, my back doesn't feel as tight."

"Or look as red," Logan added, replacing the towel. "We always hung out too long in the sun in the pool, and Mom always used this remedy. You probably won't blister, but you may still peel." He dropped the towel in the pasta pot, preparing for another application. "Sit back. You need some of this on your shoulders and upper chest."

Gingerly, she leaned against the back of the tub while he applied and reapplied the milk-soaked towel. It did seem to cool the fire on her skin. For that, she was very grateful.

But his working over her like a doctor in a MASH unit gave her another type of burn. One to her heart. While she watched him work, her gaze lingered on the angle of his jaw, the shape of his mouth, the soft wave in his hair. Her heart ached with what she had to do. She didn't know how she would be able to hand him over to another woman. Look how she ended up after the first date.

He adjusted his position on his knees and turned his body more fully toward her, his gaze locking with hers. His hand stopped patting the soothing cloth on her shoulder.

When his lips parted, her heart nearly pounded out of her chest. She trapped a breath with a quick inhale before letting it out in a tease and gentle warning. "This would look really incriminating on tape."

His gaze dropped to her mouth and then quickly rose back to her eyes, but he didn't move his hand from her shoulder. His voice dropped to a whisper. "I'll take that chance if you will."

Even through the terry cloth towel, his hand burned her more than the sun ever did. "I don't usually take chances."

"You did with the entry form for this little adventure we're on."

"I should have read the fine print," she whispered. The fire on her shoulder spread from his touch and felt hot enough to melt her bones. She curled her toes, feeling the water move and hearing it splash at her feet, as the heat continued to sizzle where he touched her.

He grinned. "Nothing like this would ever be in the fine print."

She watched his grin widen. "No, I suppose it wouldn't be."

He traced the top of her clavicle with his fingertips until he reached her neck. There, he tunneled his hand into the damp hair that brushed her shoulders.

"What are you doing?" Her words came out in a whisper.

"Changing the terms." He leaned in and inched his face toward hers.

"Why?"

The breathless question hung between them for a moment as his gaze ran over her face. "Because these past few weeks have let me see a part of you I never knew." He slid his free hand into the shallow water next to her waist and braced himself so he would not slip down onto her as he leaned so very close. "And I like it." Just as her jaw slackened and her mouth opened, he leaned forward and captured her lips with his.

Time stopped. Breathing stopped. Her heart stopped.

But she didn't stop him from kissing her and didn't want to.

She began to slide down the tub, so she wrapped her arms around Logan's neck, closed her eyes, and held on as though her life depended on it.

He reacted to her by wrapping his arms around her waist and somehow pulling both of them to their feet. For a moment, her wet feet slipped against the side of the marble tub, but he shifted one arm, scooping her out of the tub before sliding her down the length of his body until her feet touched the thick bathroom rug.

And all without breaking contact with her mouth.

"Freddy," her name was no more than a rush of breath as his hands glided down her back to the bare skin above her bathing suit near her waist. Behind them, the water in the jetted tub churned. He dropped his hand a little lower, just to the soft curve of her backside, and pulled her closer to him. "Am I hurting you? With your sunburn, I mean?" he whispered against her lips.

"What sunburn?" she whispered back against his lips.

He feathered her cheek with kisses. "I guess my mom's cure worked."

"Remind me to thank her next time I see her."

Her head spun as he trailed little kisses down her cheek to her neck. Her ability to think dulled with each touch of his lips.

She barely heard the knock on the door to her suite before the voice. "Ms. McAllister, Roberto wanted the doctor to check on your sunburn."

She put her hands on Logan's chest and pushed him back. "It's Annie. Quick, hide."

Chapter Sixteen

A soft moan of disappointment caught in Logan's throat. He stilled his hands and eased up the pressure against her body. "Annie sure has crappy timing." He looked over her shoulder toward the doorway. "And you want me to hide."

"Do you really want someone from the production crew to find you here?"

"It would definitely make things interesting." A rumble of laughter vibrated in his chest. He spun, taking her with him and trapping the back of her calves against the spa tub. "With me blocking the view from the door, someone with the right camera angle might think you have no clothes on right now. Does that sound familiar?"

She had to laugh with him. "I know I may deserve it, but as you said, crappy timing. Worry about hiding first, payback later."

He smiled just long enough to let her know hiding wouldn't be his first choice. "Okay. There'll be plenty of time to discuss revenge later. But before I go all stealth and things, I'm more interested in this."

Before she could say a word, he helped himself to another slow, hot kiss. Everything, including her ability to think, came to a screeching halt. The only thing for her to do was kiss him back.

"I guess maybe the game is on us," Logan whispered against her lips.

"We're not in it, Logan." Her heart thudded against her rib cage. Was all his attention real or just part of a script written to get higher ratings? When one show ended and the trailer for the next show aired, was Logan just giving good TV? One more kiss from him and she would breach a very precise—and so far seemingly ironclad—contract she freely signed. To accept what came with it if she did, she needed to be sure his kisses were real and not part of the production.

The knocking began again. "Ms. McAllister, are you all right?"

Freddy pulled back. "I'll be right there." She looked into Logan's eyes. "Logan, kissing is probably not a good idea right now."

His answer came in the nibbling she felt on her neck. The ability to make him stop slipped from her grasp with each touch of his lips. "But it could be about time," he said with a tilt of his head.

More kisses burned a trail across her throat. She could feel the heat of his body wherever he touched her, but she forced her brain into gear when the knocking started a third time. She pushed him away, this time with enough force to let him know she meant it.

"On my way," she called out. "And you," she pointed at Logan. "Out of sight and quiet until I tell you the coast is clear."

Logan sat down near the rack of shoes at the back of the dressing room. He could hear Freddy talking to Annie and the doctor she brought with her in the other room. He couldn't quite make out what they were saying to each other unless he got closer to the door. So he'd wait. He had no choice.

He picked up a strappy black shoe with a three-inch heel and twirled it around his forefinger. How did women walk in something like this anyway? Mesmerized, he slowed it to a lazy circle, wondering how the spiky heel might complement Freddy's long leg when she wore it. He stopped the shoe's orbit and held it as though it were Cinderella's glass slipper. He pictured the delicately arched foot encased in the leather, leading to a softly curved calf and a silk-draped thigh. The picture in his mind's eye amplified as he continued to stare at the shoe.

A smile curved his lips and he rose from the floor as silently as he could. He was having the start of a pleasant fantasy, so why not go with it?

He ran his fingers over the clothes hanging from padded hangers until he came to a rack of gowns. There he flattened his palm and slid it like a caress across each one until he found the one that felt like liquid to him. He reached up and freed it from the rack.

When he hung it on the dressing hook near the full-length mirror, it swirled like a mist before settling like the first falling of pure white snow in winter. He set the shoes under it, noticing for the first time tiny rhinestones dotting the strap that crossed the arch of the shoe.

He stepped back and crossed his arms over his chest, now picturing the dress flowing down around Freddy, the fabric settling onto her perfect curves. He could almost see the rhinestone strap of the heels arching across her foot as she walked toward him, the dress flowing around her body, accenting her thighs and the curve of her hip.

So intent, he never heard Freddy come back into the dressing room.

"Having so much fun with reality TV that you're thinking of getting cast in *Project Runway* next?" he heard her say.

"No. Being followed by cameras and miked for most of the day isn't that much fun. I thought I'd help you out."

"How so?" she asked, circling to face him.

"I found the perfect dress to go best with sunburn for tonight's elimination." He ran his hand across the pale fabric. "I don't think this material will hurt too much."

He watched her touch the delicate fabric and felt an instant pang of jealousy, wanting to feel her fingers across his skin the way they moved across the dress. He gave his head a small shake, stupefied by his reaction to the one simple gesture.

"It is soft enough," she agreed. "And strapless." She laughed. "And white doesn't clash with red."

"Speaking of which," he said, cutting his gaze to her shoulders, "you seem to be fading from bright red to a nice rosy glow."

She extended her arms and examined the color. "The doctor says I may get redder, but I think your mom's remedy worked. I feel much better. He gave me some cream to put on and told me to wear loose clothing for a while." She looked at the dress. "That qualifies."

"You're coming to elimination then?"

She nodded. "Have you seen the script?"

He blew out a long breath of air. "Wouldn't reality TV fans be surprised to know that these episodes are scripted?"

"Some maybe."

She seemed anxious for some reason, and he guessed it wasn't because of her sunburn. "What's wrong?"

"Not counting having to do this show?"

"Not counting that."

"Then nothing."

"Okay, then what's wrong with the script?"

"For you, it's great."

"And for you?"

She hesitated. "It kind of suggests you have to kiss your date."

"How does it suggest that?"

"Red letters—*Logan kisses bachelorette.*"

"That's a little more than a suggestion, Freddy."

She held her thumb and forefinger about an inch apart. "Maybe a little."

"Maybe I don't want to kiss any of the bachelorettes."

The tone of his voice made her laugh. "I can't believe we are having this conversation."

Then he laughed. "It is kind of funny."

"Maybe an on-screen kiss, complete with a script and production crew, isn't worth a Nielsen share of 9.5."

He felt a slow smile curve his mouth. "What do you think is worth it?"

He saw her eyes soften before she lowered her chin and looked at the floor while she thought about his question. Lordy, she did look beautiful, even with the creamy white skin he'd come to know over the last few weeks looking as red as a lobster. He couldn't deny it any longer, something had changed between them. He didn't think of her as merely a friend any longer. He thought of her as someone much more important. When she looked back into his eyes, he knew he had been right. A look of something more than friendship lived there now.

She shrugged her answer. "Kissing shouldn't be a viewing option. It should be reserved for a time you believe in, when you want to hold on to the moment in spite of everything," she told him. "Kissing is something special between two people and for times so deep inside you that nothing could ever dislodge the moment from your heart."

As lightly as he could, he put his hands on her arms just above her elbows and pulled her closer to him. "Do you have a moment like that inside your heart?"

"I do," she whispered.

"Can you tell me?"

Again, emotion raced around in her eyes. "No, I can't."

His gaze searched her face. "You can tell me anything." He tunneled his hands in her hair and urged her face closer to his.

He felt her heart hammering against his chest when she spoke. "Not this." Her eyes seemed dark now. Her cheeks flushed as her breath came in tight puffs that matched his own breathing.

He pulled her the last inch into his body. "It's us, isn't it?" he whispered into her ear.

She closed her eyes just before he kissed her and said, "No."

The word kicked him in the chest, but her kiss back told him that she had lied. He matched the want he felt behind her lips with every ounce of passion he could muster, hugging her into him. She'd tell him the truth, he vowed, even if it meant kissing her silly until she did.

He felt her hands splay across his chest in a gentle massage and then hesitate. Lips still on his, she opened her eyes and pressed him back.

He just stood there looking at her. He couldn't move. He had a feeling the next few minutes were going to be really important.

Chapter Seventeen

Freddy opened her mouth and then closed it again. Not because words eluded her, but for fear of what might come out. She stepped away from him, each saying nothing for the moment.

"Now tell me the truth," he urged her.

Thankfully, before she could babble out something she hoped was benign, Logan's cell phone rang. He put his hand on his pants pocket but didn't make a definitive move to answer it.

"You should take that."

"It will break the mood."

She smiled. "It already has."

Logan nodded. "We'll continue this later." He turned and dug out the cell phone from his pocket. She walked away from him as he answered.

Mesmerized, she watched him. Even dressed casually, in a white T-shirt and jeans, he looked like a man in the prime of his life: successful, driven, ready to take on anything cast at him. Her chest tightened in a lovely sensation of awe and wonder. Logan Gabriel with his endearing wit, talent, creativity, and willingness to give up a few weeks of his life to save a woman's reputation was simply the most attractive and alluring man she'd ever met.

She knew he was special when, at twelve, she started noticing boys in more than a casual way, Logan especially. As they shared their teenage years, she watched his innate sexuality emerge along with everything that comes with one's developing maturity. When she was finally ready to admit the feelings she had for him, it turned out to be too late to do anything about it. They'd become like family.

Over the next few years, they flirted a little and actually thought about dating once, but she always held back, blowing every opportunity to try to move from friend to girlfriend. The thought of stepping aside and handing him over to another woman squeezed her chest, wringing the life out of her with the impossible predicament she caused. Couple that with the fact that she loved him, completely and, maybe, foolishly, and she had no idea how she continued to breathe.

"Freddy."

Bad timing to try to tell someone you loved him when a signed contract said you had to pick his perfect match in three weeks. Of all the impulsive moves in the world, sending his picture into the magazine would haunt her more than any specter ever found on an episode of *Ghost Hunters* on Syfy.

"Freddy!"

His voice made her jump and she spun around, knocking a vase of flowers from a small table near the door. Embarrassed, she began to clean up the mess. "Sorry," she managed to get out.

Logan knelt beside her, set down his cell phone on the floor, and began helping her pick up some of the flowers. "I called out to you twice, and you didn't seem to hear me. Are you okay?"

She nodded and stood, the vase and the rest of the flowers in her hands. Another perfect moment hung in the air and then dissolved.

"Important call?" she asked him.

"Roberto. He said wardrobe has been looking all over for me. I suppose it would be better if the production staff didn't find me here. I mean, me with no shoes and you still in your bathing suit. How would that look?"

She shrugged and looked at the floor to protect herself against the pull of the attraction she felt for him. Not knowing what else to say, she said nothing.

Logan drew down his eyebrows. "Are you sure you're okay?"

She laughed. "I'm fine."

He shook his head, dismissing her reply. "It seems to me that something is wrong."

What was wrong? How about the fact that she was in love with the most eligible bachelor in the world? Logan Gabriel. A man who would be an instant celebrity once the show hit the airwaves. A man whose life she had probably changed forever with one click of the shutter on her digital camera. A man she could never tell how she felt or allow to kiss her again.

Because if he did, there would be no turning back.

"Really, I'm fine," she lied.

He walked to her, close enough to kiss her again if she would allow it. "I think we need to talk, Freddy."

"I know we do." She looked into his incredible eyes and almost closed the distance between their lips. How she managed to pull back, she did not know. "But not now. Go, and get on some fancy clothes. We have a job to do."

At the door, he paused and turned back. "You sure?"

Her stomach lurched, and again she forced the words to freeze on her lips. He didn't need to know just how not okay she really felt. "I'm good," she said with a practiced smile.

He returned the smile and winked before walking away.

Chapter Eighteen

Logan waited alone in the parlor for the elimination to begin. Try as he might, he could not seem to define what was happening or figure Freddy out any longer. He hit the rewind switch of his memory, his brows furrowing as he tried to recall every moment they'd had together and what she'd said, or rather what he thought she'd said. He needed to be sure. A wrong guess could be disastrous in the fragile game of chess they played.

"Now that's what I call tall, dark, and handsome."

The Boston accent told him he had company before he actually saw Madison. "You look nice," he said to her once she circled around and came into view.

She put one hand on his shoulder and reached with the other for one of the champagne-filled fluted glasses set on the table near him. "And you look thirsty."

He took the glass offered and stepped back. Madison's hand glided down his jacket until it rested on his chest. He sipped the champagne handed him and looked over the rim of the glass at her. She did look nice.

His gaze scanned the room, resting on each of the bachelorettes in turn. They all looked nice. Five beautiful women, each of them knowing that by the end of the night there would only be four. Then three by the end of the week and two by the week after. One of the final two would be his for a planned two-week romantic trip. He should care about which one that might be. But he didn't. He only cared about the sunburned woman who was, so far, nowhere in sight.

"You aren't here," Madison said, referring to Logan's obvious preoccupation. She refilled her glass with champagne from one of the opened bottles on the console table. "Care to tell me what you're thinking about?"

Logan declined the refill she offered him with a wave of his hand. "No, I'm here," he assured. "It's been a long day."

"Longer for those of us waiting for you to get back from your date. Did you and Jade bond?"

He offered her a polite smile. "How much bonding can one do with a camera crew following you around?"

Madison leaned back and rested her shapely backside on the backrest of one of the leather sofas. She tapped the top of her glass against her lips before speaking. "Actions speak louder than words. Take me on the next one-on-one, and I'll show you how much two people can bond in an hour or so."

"You know that isn't my decision."

She smiled. "I'm sure you can figure something out." She set her glass down on the table near her hip and walked her fingers across Logan's shoulders before looping her arm around his neck. "This can't be fun for you. Waiting to see who gets you next, I mean."

Logan could almost feel the camera zoom in on them. "And not so much fun for you either."

Madison smiled. "We cope." She glanced at the production crew filming and the makeup crew dabbing and primping. "Everyone seems occupied. Why don't we take a few minutes for ourselves and talk outside? You haven't had much time to get to know me and vice versa."

Logan weighed his options and decided that dodging questions from one bachelorette would be better than trying to avoid questions shot at him by five. He set down his glass and crooked an arm in her direction. "Where to?"

Madison smiled and slid her arm through the loop made by his. She folded her hand over his forearm. "The side patio."

Logan nodded and opened the French doors, as Madison looked over his shoulder.

Behind him, Jade caught Madison's gaze and nodded. She let the champagne glass fall from her hand. It hit the deep rich walnut flooring and shattered, sending glass shards in every direction. The rest of the bachelorettes instinctively took a step back, not wanting to get anything on their clothes or shoes. "How clumsy of me," Jade said, crouching down and appearing to clear the fragments of the very expensive crystal glass.

Logan dropped his arm, allowing Madison's hand to fall to her side, and began to walk toward Jade when the set manager stopped him. "We'll get that. You continue doing what you were going to do." Crew members were already helping with the cleanup. "Cut!" he called out. "Someone get a broom. Let's get this cleaned up so we can start filming again." The film crew turned off their equipment, and the key grip lowered the boom pole as the best boy hurried off in the direction of the kitchen.

It was exactly the reaction Jade hoped her planned awkwardness would produce.

"We're here, so let's talk," Logan said to Madison once he closed the doors to the side patio.

"What do you think of the game so far?" she asked, making herself comfortable on the seating wall. She patted the capstone. "Join me?"

Logan shook his head. "Finding love isn't a game, Madison."

"Poor choice of words on my part. What do you think of the show so far?"

"It's been interesting."

"Think of it this way. You're going on the trip of a lifetime with someone handpicked for you."

"Sounds more like an arranged marriage."

"I doubt you're thinking that far ahead."

"And I doubt you know what I'm thinking."

She pointed at him. "Exactly why we're here. You haven't been giving us your full attention." She looked up in the direction of the second floor. "We're all beginning to wonder why." She returned her gaze to Logan. "Could it be your intrepid matchmaker preoccupying you?"

Logan frowned. "Freddy and I have known each other for a long time."

"In what capacity?" Madison pressed.

"We grew up together. Sort of. We've known each other since we were kids." He eyed her almost angrily. "And I would imagine that you all know by now that Freddy and I are close."

"We know you have a relationship of some sort, but we can't quite seem to figure it out yet."

"Have you spent some time with Freddy?"

"We have." Madison lifted her chin. "She got quite a nasty sunburn today."

"How long were you with her?"

"A few hours."

Madison looked rather tan. He felt annoyance well inside him remembering the pain Freddy's sunburn caused her. He knew the proverbial "All's fair in love and war," but if Madison purposely kept Freddy baking in the sun to keep her from showing up at elimination, then war it would be.

"And not a sunspot on you," he said, forcing a smile.

"So glad you noticed," Madison returned.

Logan nodded once.

"I do hope Freddy will feel up to coming to elimination tonight," Madison said after a lengthy silence.

"Well, since she's my eyes and ears around here, I hope so, too."

"Your eyes and ears. Interesting. But your eyes and ears are not exactly what we ladies are interested in." She stood. Reaching out, she placed the palms of her hands on his shoulders. She leaned forward, her mouth next to his ear. "So watch out, Mr. Eligible Bachelor, because I am pretty sure this little game we're all playing is about to change."

Chapter Nineteen

"Ms. McAllister! You've done it this time."

Roberto's voice boomed through the doorway of Freddy's upstairs suite. She'd never heard him speak this loud before. Not a good sign.

She'd spun to face him. "What have I done?"

Eyes narrowed and lips pressed together to form a thin line, Roberto strode into the room. Annie followed, holding a laptop. He gestured for Annie to put it on the nearest table and shoed her away from it.

"Look here."

He pressed the Enter key, and the home page for a popular online e-zine covering reality TV appeared. The first headline read, "*Eligible Bachelor* Spoilers."

Freddy's brow wrinkled. She read the area to which Roberto pointed: "News and rumors for the upcoming new reality show. Cast Members. Blog. Scandal in the making."

"What's this?" she asked. "What's a spoiler?"

Annie took over. "A spoiler is when someone inside leaks something about the show. Usually spoilers are released after the show airs, but someone leaked it now. And we still have a good three weeks' filming to do."

"That's what makes this so bad," Roberto added. "The network could yank the whole thing. I mean why watch the show if the outcome is already all over the Internet?"

Freddy opened her mouth to respond and then closed it when Roberto clicked on the link to the website. A picture of her and Logan popped up.

Roberto began reading. "Is *Eligible Bachelor* over before it starts? That's the question some people are asking as an intimate video surfaced yesterday. Are Logan Gabriel, *Elan Magazine*'s Most Eligible Bachelor contest winner, and his longtime friend, Frederika McAllister, the woman who will pick his dream date, more than just friends? The clip shows the hunky bachelor and Frederika entering one of the pool houses after shooting an episode for the show. They did not come out for quite a while, leaving some to wonder if the contest is even real. Watch the video, and judge for yourself. The clip is time-stamped to show how long they stayed inside. You can hear voices coming from inside the cabana during the filming, but you can't make out what is being said. Or being done. Then take our poll after you watch, and let us know your thoughts."

"There's a poll?" Freddy asked weakly.

"Care to see the results to date?" Roberto asked, aiming the cursor at the prompt.

"I suppose I'm going to whether I want to or not."

"You are." Roberto logged in next to the answer that indicated the responder who chose this particular selection thought the whole show was staged. When the graph appeared showing the vote total, it looked like a majority of the responders did also. "There you have it. We're ruined."

Think, Freddy, her mind screamed. *Talk yourself out of this or be prepared to have your wages attached from a lawsuit settlement for the rest of your life and probably the next.*

"It's not so bad," she managed to get out.

Roberto crossed his arms over his chest. "And what were *you* watching." He dropped his arms, letting his shoulders sink. "I'm finished."

"No," Freddy said, swiping her hand in the air. "Not at all." She hoped she sounded more convincing than she felt.

"What went on in there?"

Roberto's grim voice shattered the last vestige of confidence Freddy had gathered around her. "Nothing," she assured. It was a lie, but not a very big one. Much like the kiss they shared—a kiss, but not a very passionate one. "We talked. That's all."

"That's all?"

"It's not very private around here with people lurking with cameras, and boom mikes appearing from trees." She put her hands on her hips. "We talked. Is that so bad?"

Roberto pointed to the laptop screen. "Depends on the spin."

"Nothing happened," she repeated. *Although, I would have liked something more.*

"Nothing better have." He spaced his thumb and forefinger an inch apart and stuck it near her face. "From today on, someone is going to be this close to you at all times."

She could see the anger on his face, framed by his fingers. "Okay. I get it."

"I will not lose the network spot." He glared at Freddy. "I don't have to remind you about the contract you signed, do I?"

"For the thousandth time, no."

"So then we agree."

Freddy drew down her brows. "On what?"

She saw triumph run across Roberto's face. "That I'm in charge."

She shrugged her answer. "I guess."

"And being in charge, here's my decision. You will post a comment on the web."

"Okay. Facebook or Twitter?"

"It's beyond that. Staff has started an *Eligible Bachelor* counterblog—*EB* for short. You'll be posting to it regularly over the course of the series."

"I will?"

"You or your designated ghostwriter, Annie, will. I trust her, and you'll have to trust her as well. She'll discuss the postings with you before they go up."

"Okay." The word came out more like a question, since Freddy suspected more was coming.

"And she will guide the posting in a way that will add to the show's drama, depending on the ratings we had for the week. Are we clear on that, Ms. McAllister?"

She looked at the laptop screen and then back at Roberto. He was trying to turn her to stone with his glare. She sighed. "What am I supposed to post today?"

Roberto held out his right hand, and Annie slipped a sheet of paper into it. He handed it to Freddy. "Word for word." He motioned to the laptop. "Now type."

The look that crossed Roberto's eyes told Freddy she had no choice. In her best two-fingered hunt-and-peck, she read the statement as she typed it onto the *EB* blog:

Hi. I'm Freddy McAllister, Logan's friend and designated cupid-helper for the series. If you're reading this, you're curious about the rumors already swirling around Eligible Bachelor, *even though we haven't even finished taping yet.*

Where do these leaks come from anyway?

I'd like to set the record straight. Logan and I are here for the same reason—to find his perfect match. And let me tell you straight up, it's not me. I should know; I've known Logan since I was twelve.

I'm sure there will be more rumors and innuendo as the show progresses. I hope you'll come back often for the real truth, along with a look behind the scenes and inside life here at the mansion.

Gotta run. We're having elimination in an hour.

Cheers—Freddy

She rested her hands in her lap.

"Now hit enter, Ms. McAllister." When she did, a satisfied smile replaced Roberto's glower. "I trust we will have no more covert rendezvous?"

She nodded in agreement.

"So we understand each other then?"

She nodded again.

"Good." At the door he paused and turned back to face her. "And I also trust tonight's elimination will be as entertaining as possible."

She tossed her hand in the air. "Anything for ratings."

With an exaggerated smile of approval, Roberto left.

Annie didn't.

"I can get dressed by myself," Freddy assured her.

"I'm sure you can," Annie replied, "but from now on, you're not doing much by yourself, so you better get used to having me around."

"What are you two doing out here?" Lori stepped out onto the terrace and joined Logan and Madison. "Not plotting to keep yourself on for another month, are you, Madison?"

Madison raised the champagne glass to her lips and looked at Lori over the rim before finishing the champagne in one long drink. She put the empty glass on the stone cap of the patio wall. "I believe we all are plotting something in one way or another."

Lori walked to Logan and looped her arm around his waist. "Then I need a few minutes with Logan to state my own case."

Not to be outdone, Madison placed her hand on his shoulder. He saw the women exchange rather venomous looks. "I'm not worried," Madison replied.

Logan barely listened as they swapped clipped barbs and veiled remarks like two kids, each trying to get the other to back down and say "uncle." His mind contrasted each of them with Freddy. She had depth of character, while Lori's and Madison's personas seemed to run only as deep as the makeup on their faces. Freddy was honest and caring, concerned about the consequences of her actions toward other people; Lori and Madison were more concerned with being here another week.

Madison glared at Lori. "And why are you out here?"

"The crew cleaned up the glass, and I believe they need us inside. They want to start taping again," she replied in a sickly sweet voice.

Logan had had enough. The venom being exchanged in glares and words was enough to bring down a bear. He stepped out of the dual embraces and opened the French doors leading inside. "Then we shouldn't keep the production crew waiting."

Freddy thought her head would explode when she saw Logan walk into the room with Lori and Madison, their arms looped around his waist. He smiled when he saw her, and she had to grab the back of one of the leather chairs to keep from running to him. He looked so incredible in the dark suit he wore. She hoped he didn't hear her sharp intake of breath when she saw him. Though she couldn't be sure, she felt it must have boomed in the room as loud as it had in her ears.

He untangled himself from the bachelorettes. "Hi," he said, reaching her and letting his gaze run slowly down her length. "You wore the dress I put out." His gaze rose to her eyes. "You look hot."

"So do you."

He gestured to her shoulders. "What happened to the bathing suit lines?"

"Makeup."

"Nice job."

She smiled, and so did he. It nearly became her undoing. She couldn't seem to control herself and reached up and touched his shoulder. She felt his muscles tense underneath the high-end suit fabric. He closed his eyes for a moment, as if enjoying the touch as much as she was. Almost at the same time, she realized she couldn't let the camera crew catch any of it.

"Lint," she whispered, brushing the fictional material from his shoulder.

He leveled her a hard look, as though she'd awoken him from a pleasant dream. "You're thinking about lint?"

She grinned in an exaggerated smile. "And about making sure that everything is perfect for TV."

Just as the ensuing silence began to feel solid around them, Roberto walked into the room, Annie on his heels. He clapped to get everyone's attention. "People, we're ready to begin taping the elimination." He turned to the cameraman. "Get a shot of Logan mingling with the bachelorettes. We'll open with that and then cut to a shot of Freddy entering." He turned to Freddy. "You go out into the hall, and make a grand entrance like the matchmaker you're supposed to be."

She glanced at Logan. He as looked unhinged as she felt.

In the hallway, she didn't think she could stand it much longer as she watched the women surround him. She had to detach from the situation. She closed her eyes and sighed. She could do this. For the darn contract. For him. She put her hands over her face and whispered the words that had been echoing inside her brain since Roberto had left her upstairs.

"What in the world am I going to do?"

Chapter Twenty

"You're going to finish this, that's what you're going to do."

Freddy spun around and saw Annie standing behind her.

"Think of it this way," Annie added. "In a few weeks, he'll be back from his dream date and free to do whatever he wants." She smiled. "With whomever he wants to do it, so stick to the script, and you'll be fine. I think everything you've done so far can be edited into a pretty interesting show."

Freddy exhaled loudly through her nose. "I'm not so sure about that."

"I've done some reality TV before being hired on for *EB*, and we have some of the best editors in the business. Trust me, this show is going to be great. When you analyze what's happened, what's been slowly revealed in the shows we have in the can, and add what can be surmised by the viewers, it's going to be pretty amazing."

Freddy shrugged. "I guess anything can get tweaked."

Annie snickered. "Yeah, tweaked. Is that what they're calling it now?"

"I don't speak editing."

Annie lifted one arched eyebrow as she sat on one of the chairs in the hallway, indicating for Freddy to do the same. "You don't have to speak editing to see what I see."

Freddy tilted her head. "What do you mean?"

"The game playing and the great clothes you all get to wear, that's all fine, but let's face it, you're in love with Logan."

Freddy turned the surprise she felt into a laugh. "No, I'm not," she denied.

"You're in love, all right. I can see it every time you're with him." Annie crossed her arms with an air of satisfaction. "Most of the crew agrees."

Freddy frowned. "Even Roberto?"

"This is Roberto's first foray into directing. He's more concerned with the ratings than with what's going on right in front of his nose."

As Annie stared at her, Freddy felt her face warm. Fortunately, she knew her skin was red enough to hide the blush that undoubtedly accompanied the heat. She wondered exactly what Annie and the crew did see. She thought she'd kept her affection for Logan hidden in public, but maybe not.

"You know, I've known Logan for a very long time," Freddy said in a rush of breath. "There may be something between us, but certainly he doesn't love me."

Annie tipped her head and shot Freddy a calculating look. "Frankly, I'm thrilled about the way things are going. It will be quite the finale."

"How do you know that?"

"I feel it."

Freddy shook her head. "I get another type of feeling when Roberto threatens lawsuits. A high-profile lawsuit would ruin Logan's reputation and his career. I won't risk that."

"I wouldn't worry too much. If the rest of the show goes how I think it might, *EB* could get nominated for an Emmy."

"But it hasn't even aired yet."

Annie tapped her temple with her forefinger. "In here it has, and it's a helluva ending."

Freddy opened her mouth to respond, then closed it after scrutinizing the woman across from her. The touch of devil in Annie's eyes made Freddy mull over everything she'd said. And then things began to gel. "You somehow knew I had feelings for Logan right from the beginning, didn't you?"

"Guilty."

"And you somehow had a hand in picking us for this show, too, didn't you?"

Annie's smile was sly. "Guilty again."

"You were the one who put up the spoilers."

"I can't take all the credit. I did have some help."

Only one word escaped Freddy's lips. "Why?"

"There's a ton of dating shows on air, especially on cable. I wanted this one to be different, more emotional. I read your application, and I could feel how much you cared for him right on the paper. Then I met you the first day filming, and I knew you two were perfect—for the show and for each other. Toss in an impossible situation with forced seclusion in a beautiful mansion, a few beautiful women to bring out both the insecurity and the jealousy, and presto, you have the perfect setting for drama and emotion."

Freddy felt the blood rush from her head, sure even her sunburned skin was now a nice pasty white. She gripped the arms of her chair. This was a setup right from the start, a scheme to trap her into admitting her feelings for Logan on camera in front of millions of viewers for the ultimate ratings sweep. When the editors pieced together the film to heighten the suspense for each episode, those same viewers would push *EB* to the number one spot. And as long as the producer and director decided let the situation unravel and then build to an emotional climax, it would probably stay there.

It was both brilliant and horrible. Freddy shifted in the chair as the right words eluded her. A tendril of anger curled around her throat, cutting off an angry retort. "Does Logan know about any of this?" she managed to whisper.

"No. It's better that way. Scheming women play better on camera than conniving men."

"I'm not a scheming woman."

"Aren't you? You did send in his picture without his knowledge. You must have been planning something."

"Nothing as sordid as what you are planning."

"Nonetheless, it seems like we are a team now."

"Do I have a choice?"

"No."

Freddy fought to contain her annoyance. She didn't have a choice. Though she hated being used for ratings, she reluctantly had to admit she had also tried to use the photo contest to her own advantage. Now Logan's career had gotten tied to the show, with the winning bachelorette starring in his ad campaign. What a nightmare. This could only be payback for that.

"I'll finish the show, but not because of your threats. I'll finish it because it will cement Logan's career in advertising."

Annie dismissed the protest with a wave of her hand. "Whatever, as long as you finish."

Annie's indifference made Freddy pause. Maybe she and Logan were perfect for each other, but that train had left the station a long time ago. Maybe she had let her fantasies show on her face in a weak moment, but she wouldn't allow that to have any bearing on how she was going to get to the end of this nightmare she had created. Logan's career was at stake, not to mention both their reputations, all signed and sealed by a contest entry she hadn't bothered to read.

"Logan and I have known each other for so many years. We're like family."

"Not any family I know," Annie said, shaking her head in disagreement. "In fact, I don't think we could have picked two more perfectly attuned people to kick off the inaugural season."

Freddy frowned. "Logan and I are not attuned." She began counting off on her fingers. "We have opposite goals, opposite interests. I want commitment, he wants freedom."

"Lucky for me and *EB* that opposites attract." Annie stared Freddy dead straight in her eyes. "And you should consider yourself lucky that we are giving you a way out of a whole bunch of trouble by finishing the series in a way that will make us all happy."

The sensation of being manipulated bubbled inside Freddy along with her anger. "Happy? How do you make someone happy by forcing them into an impossible situation?"

"I didn't. You did." Annie's voice was so tight that she practically hissed. "So finish it, and let come what may."

She started to say more, but then put her hand to her ear. She looked away from Freddy, obviously listening to a voice coming from the earpiece she wore.

"Five minutes," she said when she looked back at Freddy. "I suggest you use that time to compose yourself and figure out which of our lovely contenders is going home and which will have the next one-on-one date." At the door, she stopped. "And remember, do it all as if your future depended on the outcome, because it does,"

After the elimination, Freddy sat on the tiled pool edge, splashing her feet in the cold water. The night air chilled her, but she didn't care. She welcomed the cold air on her hot skin. She didn't know how she ever got through the filming, but somehow she did and with the flair expected. Lori went home, and Madison would have

Logan all to herself tomorrow for a night on the town. Confident that Logan would see through the preppie's smug personality and not let her get too attached, Freddy thought the date should be harmless enough.

Make a list, Freddy thought to herself. After tonight, Careelyn would go and then Madison. Was that the right order for elimination? But that left Jade and Stacy. She didn't like that combination.

Okay then, so Jade next, then Madison, leaving Careelyn and Stacy—the beauty queen and the teacher. Not a great combo there either. Most of the audience would probably be pulling for the teacher.

She ran though other combinations in her head. The beauty queen and the preppie. The preppie and the teacher. She sighed hard and long, each combination its own horror sideshow for Annie to play up for sweeps week.

The blood pumping wildly inside her ears turned into a screaming white noise that deafened her to most of the sounds around her. She almost didn't hear the sound of someone clearing his throat. Then she heard it again.

Freddy didn't have to look up to know who stood there. "Hi, Logan."

He sat beside her and took off his shoes and socks before rolling up his pants to his knees and slipping his feet into the water. "This seems to be our meeting place."

"What are you doing?" she asked him. "Shouldn't you and Madison be getting to know each other better?"

"We can do that tomorrow. It's you I'm concerned about."

Freddy looked down at her feet. "Don't be." She looked at him, feeling utterly miserable. He did look concerned. "Logan, I have really made a mess of things. This has been a setup from the beginning. Annie caught me between takes and…" She stopped. It would do no good to tell him the truth. He might try to do something gallant, and she couldn't have that. *Keep with the plan,* she told herself. *One foot in front of the other until you get to the end.* "And she wants to make sure that we have enough drama to stay in the number one spot all the way to the finale." She knew the night would hide the fact that all the blood had probably drained from her head, leaving her face a ghostly white color in the process.

"Is that why you chose Madison for tomorrow's date?"

Freddy nodded.

"You know she's not my type."

Frustration made Freddy reach into the water and send a healthy splash at him. He still had athletic reactions and managed to dodge most of it.

"Hey!" he shouted, running his fingers through his hair. "What was that all about?"

"I have more to worry about than your type, whatever that is." She scrunched her face and announced in a singsong voice, "I have to pick you the perfect date."

"You don't have to do this." Logan's voice was surprisingly low and calm, despite him looking almost angry to her.

"Of course I do. We both know the show must go on."

Behind them, they heard movement, and both turned toward the sound. They saw a cameraman with a handheld filming them. The cameraman waved back when they acknowledged him.

"See," Freddy said, gesturing to the crew member. "He is the insurance policy that we do exactly what we're supposed to do." She adjusted her position and put a foot of space between her and Logan.

In a fluid motion, he compensated, closing the distance to where it had been before the cameraman appeared.

"What are you doing?"

"Making a point. I'm not going to let Eyes back there govern my every move. If I want to sit next to you, I'll sit next to you. I don't care what it looks like after an edit."

Freddy bit down on her lip. "You're mad at me."

He gestured over his shoulder. "No. I'm mad at camera boy back there."

"He's just doing his job. I got you into this mess."

"But together, we'll get out of it." He reached out and patted her hand. "It's been fun, and we should at least have fun while we're here."

"Fun?" The word fell from Freddy's lips like a rock being dropped from the top of a mountain. How was she supposed to have fun when she would have to hand Logan over to another woman? "You just want to have fun?"

"Sure. Why not? The mansion. The sets. The scripts. Why should anything have to change? I've had some fun so far, haven't you?"

Freddy felt her stomach go cold. "Of course. That's what it's all about. The bachelorettes having fun, the audience having fun." She stood, sending water droplets all around as she pulled her feet from the water and looked down at Logan. "In the morning, you can start by having some more no-strings-attached fun with one beautiful lady. Then in a day or two, it will be on to the next one. You can dabble with each of them because it's all in a contract that says anything goes because it's just plain fun."

Logan quickly rose and joined her, putting his hand on her arm. "Freddy, that's not what I meant."

She looked down at his hand before looking back up into his eyes. "Of course it is." She hoped her expression was neutral as she shrugged her arm free. "I need to go over tomorrow's schedule." She started to walk away.

"Freddy, wait."

She turned back. "See you tomorrow after your date. I'm sure it will be...fun."

Chapter Twenty-One

She misunderstood me, Logan thought as he watched Freddy walk away. He had to talk to her and explain. But his feet seemed rooted in concrete. He'd been so preoccupied with the cameraman behind them that he hadn't thought about what he'd been saying.

It's been fun.

What an idiot.

He'd made it sound as though he'd been playing along without a thought to anyone's feelings. That wasn't what he'd meant at all.

He jogged back to the mansion and ripped open the front door. Steering clear of the wing where the bachelorettes stayed, he searched everywhere for Freddy but only ran into some of the production crew. They hadn't seen her either, and she wasn't in her suite.

He ran outside and sprinted down the front stairs. A dark movement ahead in the driveway caught his eye. Was that her?

"Freddy!" he called out.

He saw the figure stop and look back before walking again. It was her. He took off running and caught up with her in less than a minute. She stopped when he reached her.

"Where are you going?"

"For a walk to clear my head."

"Can I come along?"

Lifting her chin, she pushed some hair from her eyes. "I think your head is clear enough."

She started walking again, and he matched her stride. "I didn't mean what I said back at the pool."

"It's okay. I understand. It's the situation. Nothing is real here. The fabulous house, the dates, they are all props. Even us. We're just like actors playing a part." She tossed her head. "You were right. We shouldn't take it so seriously and just have fun."

He reached for her, but she stepped back. "Some things are real. We can figure out which ones together."

"What is there to figure out? I entered a contest, and I won. You won. We get to stay at a fabulous mansion for a few weeks, during which time we have everything a person could ever want or need. And you have even more. You've had the full attention of six beautiful women here."

"Seven," he corrected.

She shook her head. "That's flattering, Logan, but I'm not in that count."

"You are beautiful, Freddy."

She looked at the ground and shook her head. "Doesn't the fact that you still call me Freddy even though we're not kids any longer tell you something?"

"It tells me that we're close."

"Like family?"

He felt as puzzled as he probably looked. "Maybe closer than family." He watched emotion play across her face and felt he had just lost something precious. "Freddy, I…"

She raised her hand. "I know. I think I've known from the beginning, but just didn't admit it."

"Known?"

She nodded and gestured to the mansion. "It's all just a dream, the same one every girl has when she thinks about finding her

Prince Charming. But, this time, the fantasy is bigger because there are six of them all rolled into one."

"Not seven?"

Again, she shook her head. "Besides, these shows don't have a very good track record when it comes to making dreams come true."

"But people keep trying, and maybe we should, too."

"When the show is over, so is the fantasy."

"What about the two people who end up together?"

"It's especially hard for them. The show tapes way in advance and," she raised her eyebrows, "the contract is pretty specific about secrecy. The couple can't even be together until the last show airs and everyone gets back together for the tell-all reunion. That time period has proven to take its toll on even the most determined couple."

"But we've shared so much these past few weeks."

"We're not a couple, Logan." She inhaled deeply, and her voice broke. "What we shared was for the show. We played our parts well, and still are. I'll always be Freddy to you. All these years, nothing happened between us. A few weeks of forced interaction are not going to change that." She smiled. "We're friends, Logan. That's all we should ever be."

"Are you sure that's how you feel?"

She glanced down before looking up into his eyes. "You know I'm right."

Was she? Could he have been caught up in the romanticism of the TV show and all the glitz the producers threw at him? Was she right that if something would have happened between them, it would have happened a long time ago? What he felt, was it real or reality TV? He drew her to him and rested his chin on her forehead. There was no script that told either of them how to act now.

And that just might cost both of them the chance to find out.

She pulled back slightly and lifted on tiptoes, kissing him on the cheek. "You go on back to the mansion. I need to finish my walk."

"Alone?"

She ran her hands down his arm and took his hands in hers. "I have to figure out which one of the remaining ladies is going on that dream date with you. I think I need to do that alone." She took s few steps away and then turned back. She put her fingers to her lips and blew him a kiss. "See ya, Logman."

Logan watched her until the driveway turned to the right and she slipped out of sight.

For the first time in a very long time, he felt out of control. Was she right? Did he get caught up in the adventure, the excitement? Had his own ego taken over once he was semialone with six beautiful women who were required to do nothing but hang on his every word until the show ended and he ended up with one of them?

And what about Freddy? Were his feelings real and growing each time he was with her, or was it just all part of the game?

Think, he commanded himself. *Figure it out, and fast.* Whatever conclusion he came to would ultimately affect a whole lot of hearts. He owed it to Freddy, to the bachelorettes, and to himself.

Chapter Twenty-Two

The next two weeks at the mansion were heart-shredding for Freddy. Her stomach churned from too much anxiety trying to avoid Logan, and her head throbbed with too many sleepless nights trying to figure out the least disturbing way to make it to the end.

One by painful one, the bachelorettes dwindled to the final two. Now with only Jade and Madison left in the mansion, Freddy tried not to agonize too much over the final dates he had with each one. After all that had happened, Roberto didn't trust her picking out Logan's perfect match, so he had changed the ending. Now Logan had to select the woman for him from the two left.

While the production crew buzzed getting the mansion ready for the final episode, she busied herself with packing. Right after the final taping, she planned on leaving.

Trying to avoid spending any more time with Logan than necessary had been both difficult and painful. Fortunately, with Annie nearly attached at her hip, there hadn't been too many opportunities anyway. Once she got home, the plan would be to dye her hair, buy some new clothes, and forget all about Logan Gabriel and *Eligible Bachelor*.

Provided, of course, that the tabloids and TV newsmagazines left her alone. Depending on the editing, they might be sitting on her doorstep every day. She hoped the boring and automatic, almost robotic, performance she'd managed to evoke over the last few tapings would take care of that. She'd purposefully faded into the background, preferring to act like scenery instead of taking much of an active part in the show. The bachelorettes took the cue and filled in rather nicely, creating some drama of their own, floating conspiracy theories, and jostling for position when Logan was around.

At this point, she did not care which way the show went once aired. She only wanted to get it over with. She wasn't ready to face a world without Logan in it every minute, as he had been since they'd arrived. They had spent more time together in the last few weeks than they had since Pee Wee football camp. Despite the obstacles and the rules, it had only made her want more. More time, more Logan.

But she mailed that darned entry and nothing had worked out the way she thought it would. She should have never messed with providence; she should simply have let nature take its course. You can't force someone to feel something that doesn't come naturally. She knew that now. Lesson learned, albeit it a little too late.

Her stomach managed to both lurch and growl at the same time. She hadn't eaten all day. There had to be some crackers in the kitchen. She opened the door and stuck her head out into the hallway. All clear.

Quickly, she cleared the balcony landing and raced down the stairs. She had just turned the corner and entered the kitchen when a hand grabbed her wrist. She jerked her head. Logan stood next to her.

"Back from your final date with Jade so soon?"

"We finished taping about an hour ago."

She walked to the sink and ran the water before opening the cabinet and retrieving a glass. "How was it?"

"A bit awkward," he admitted.

Freddy forced a laugh. "How awkward could an all-expenses-paid date with a beautiful woman be?"

"Depends what's underneath the pleasant appearance."

She shrugged. "So then you'd rather I chose Madison as your dream girl." She took a healthy drink to keep her from saying any more.

"You sound angry."

"I'm not." She opened the freezer and fetched a few ice cubes. She placed them in the glass before refilling it.

Logan stopped her from walking by him with a hand to her arm. "Ah, could you give me a hint what's going on inside that mind of yours, since I've proven myself to be a lousy mind reader."

She glared at him before catching herself and softening her features. In his eyes, she could see her worst nightmare—it showed a man with more on his mind than wondering what was on hers. "Nothing. It's nothing." She smiled. "Gotta run. Got a lot of packing to do." She saw his eyes take on a strange intensity as he spoke.

"I've missed spending time with you over the last few days, Freddy."

She threw up her hands, spun around, and leaned against the counter, a careful distance between them. "For some reason, you aren't listening to me."

"Explain it to me again then."

When he made a move toward her, she put up her hand. "Stay right there. Things started to get all messed up the last time we were alone together in this kitchen."

"I know."

She could feel a mortifying heat climb up her throat and knew a bright red color probably accompanied it. He agreed that their relationship was a mess. The last ray of hope left alive inside her flickered out.

She took a deep breath and began. "You saw the way your boss salivated when he thought about all the free airtime for your firm. He's probably already ordered the nameplate for your new office."

"He did love the ad campaign twist."

"And you're about to go on the adventure of a lifetime, and I hope it's good for you in every way."

"Every way?"

She nodded, and her heart climbed to somewhere in her throat. She had hoped that, along the way, a lightbulb would go on in Logan's head and he would understand that the two of them were and always had been special together. She had hoped to hear him tell her how much he cared for her, maybe even realize that he loved her.

But she had tried to force him into it by trapping him in this reality show. She couldn't do it any longer. If anything started here, it would certainly end when the fantasy ended. And that would be both disastrous and uncomfortable.

She couldn't survive without him in her life in some way. She'd rather have him as a friend than nothing at all. She needed to finish this. Now. Settle it, and send him on his way so she could survive what came next.

She braced herself for what had to be said. "I'll always be there for you, Logan." Her heart seemed to be coiling tighter inside her chest. "As your friend."

Logan shifted away from her. "So you're ready to send me off to paradise with either Madison or Jade?"

Not trusting herself to speak, Freddy nodded.

"Okay then. I understand. Let's do it." He touched her on the arm and left the kitchen.

As she watched him leave, her mind screamed for him to come back, though no words escaped her lips. He understood nothing, and she was back at square one with nowhere else to go.

"I can do this," she whispered, though her heart ached and her head began to throb. "I want you to be happy." Her breath caught, and she said what she should have said a long time ago. "Because I love you."

Logan stood in the hallway just outside the kitchen, Freddy's voice hitting him like a sledgehammer in his chest. She loved him?

His first thought was to go in and ask her. But what if he was wrong? He knew she loved him, but what if it was the way she loved chocolate or her mom's meatloaf? Loved him. Not *loved him*.

There was only one way to find out for sure. He needed to talk to Roberto.

Chapter Twenty-Three

On set in the massive foyer of the mansion, Freddy saw the cameraman press his hand to his ear, probably listening to a set of final instructions. Logan must have made his final choice, and he and his date were on their way here now.

She had managed to get through the last two weeks by doing everything by the book, or rather, according to the script. She blogged every night, the *EB* blog sprouting cyberwings and gaining more than a million followers. Redemption in the eyes of Roberto, or so he said. The show was already a huge success, and it hadn't aired one episode yet.

The script Annie had handed her a few minutes ago said that after the selection, Logan and the lady of his dreams would stop by for some final words from her before continuing on their way. One more shot to her heart and it would be all over. She winced. Maybe in more ways than one.

"Five minutes, Ms. McAllister," the set director called, as the hairstylist made some final adjustments to the curls in her hair.

Five minutes and the show would be officially over. Her hands went cold, and she thought about turning and running, but she knew she had to finish. She pasted on a smile and waited.

When the front door opened, she felt her smile fade with the surprise. "Roberto, what are you doing here?"

"Change of plans," he replied, signaling to the crew. "We're moving to poolside to film the final scene." He took her by the arm and guided her out the front door.

"I'm confused." She kept pace with him as he walked double-time toward the back. "Why the change?"

"In a nutshell, I fired Annie. That means we need to change the ending again."

Freddy stopped. "You fired Annie?"

Three strides ahead of her, Roberto motioned for her to keep walking. "Yes," he said when she caught up. "I found out Annie leaked the spoilers."

"Really? Why?"

Roberto's annoyance came out in a harsh sigh. "Because she could. But she had help."

"Who? A cameraman?"

"No, Jade."

Freddy thought she felt her jaw drop to the ground and reached up to check if it was still attached to her face. "You're kidding?"

Roberto shook his head. "I'm as serious as a heart attack, which I almost had by the way, when I saw Annie passing Jade a flash drive. When I confronted Jade, she broke down and confessed that Annie promised to make sure she would be the last one standing in exchange for helping leak information. Come to find out Jade's brother is the owner of DontLook.com, the site where the spoilers are posted. One of the cameramen helped by getting the video onto the drive. He's gone, too."

"But Annie was so into the show and the ratings. Why would she do that?"

"Because if I failed, she thought she would step right in."

"I guess it makes sense."

"Only if you are a backstabbing witch."

"So you changed the show's ending so Annie couldn't totally sabotage the show." She paused. "But since Jade is gone, that means only Madison is left."

Roberto looked at his watch. "Yes, and we need to hurry to wrap this up. The crew is filming Logan's final scene with Madison, and I only have the mansion rented for another thirty minutes." He reached out and fluffed her hair. "That will have to do. Now get out there."

"Okay, okay, already," Freddy said, half walking, half stumbling onto the pool deck. She regained her footing and smoothed the front of her gown. "I got it. I'm ad-libbing my enthusiasm for the preppie." Roberto shooed her forward with both hands as the boom lights came on. She turned toward the camera and stopped. Logan was already in place.

And he was alone.

"Hey, Freddy!"

She stood at the edge of the pool tile, her mouth in the shape of the last word she'd said, her eyes just as wide. She felt the color drain from her face and then rush back. Giving her head a small shake, she walked toward him. "Where's your date?"

"She's here, don't worry."

"I'm not worried. I just want to get this over with." She stood next to him and faced the camera while Roberto set up the shot. "Did you hear about Annie?"

He nodded while a makeup artist patted his forehead with a sponge. "Who would have guessed she wanted to submarine the show."

She looked around. "What are we supposed to do? I'm kinda used to following the script, and there is none for this."

"I know, isn't it great?"

She shrugged. "I suppose." She noticed he held the Bio-Shoes in one hand. "Did you forget to give them to your new model-slash-date?"

"No."

Logan's reply was cut short by Roberto. "And here we go in five, four, three…" He signed the last two numbers.

From the shadows, the show's host emerged from the pathway leading to the pool, and the cameraman swiveled to get the shot.

Freddy leaned toward Logan. "Someone cut off my earpiece. What is he saying?"

Logan shushed her with a finger to his lips. "It will be over in a minute."

The host walked to them, his words becoming clearer. "And while this started out as a chance for Logan Gabriel to meet the woman of his dreams, Logan tells me that the experience here at the mansion proved to him that he had already met her a long time ago." He gestured, directing the camera shot to Logan and Freddy. "Logan," he prompted, "it's all yours."

Logan reached out and took Freddy's hand. It was the first time he'd touched her in weeks, and the contact sent a shock wave through him.

"You look great," he said.

"So do you." Her brows furrowed. "What is going on here? You're supposed to be choosing your perfect date."

"Something like that," Logan replied with a soft laugh.

"I'm glad it worked out for you."

For a long moment, she just stared at him, trying so hard to keep her composure that he could see the struggle in her eyes. "Everything worked out, but not the way I thought it would when this whole thing was sprung on me at my office." He winked. "But work out it did."

"I'm happy for you." She took a step back and tried to pull her hand free, but he held on tight.

"Freddy, I need to tell you something."

"No, you don't." She leaned toward him and lowered her voice to a whisper. "You need to tell the viewers about your date so I can get out of here."

"I'm trying to do just that."

"Then get on with it," she said through clenched teeth. "I want to go home."

"You can't go home."

"Why not?"

"Ready for it?"

"I am," she said in a singsong voice.

He mimicked her. "You sure?"

"I'm sure."

"Wait for it," he drew the last word out so long that it sounded as though it could have been four syllables.

She dropped her shoulders, the words coming out in a rush of air. "For crying out loud, I'm dying here. Will you get this over with already?"

He said nothing, only handed her the shoes.

"What am I supposed to do with these?" she asked, taking one in each hand.

Logan felt his smile break free. "Put them on, because I've chosen you."

Chapter Twenty-Four

Chills cartwheeled down Freddy's spine. "Wrong answer, player." She thrust the shoes into Logan's stomach. "Hell's bells, this isn't a joke, Logan."

He pushed them back at her. "I'm not joking."

She hit him in the arm with the left one. "Then you're just trying to make good TV for Roberto."

"Are you saying that I'm using you, Freddy? Don't you trust me more than that?"

"Of course I trust you. But I also trust that you know your career hangs in the balance, and I need you to do the right thing, so try another answer, or risk the consequences."

"But I'm serious. I pick you."

She sighed. This time angrily. Clearly, he had forgotten the consequences. "Unemployment won't exactly support the lifestyle you are used to."

"I'm not unemployed."

She held the shoes in front of his face. "You will be if you don't fill these."

"I'm trying to, Freddy."

"Okay then." She lowered her hands. "Tell Madison to get out here then, and quit kidding around."

"Madison is on her way home in a taxi."

Freddy's mouth fell open. She sighed heavily and looked down at the shoes in her hands. "Great, so now what are you going to do with these?"

"This." He took the shoes and chucked them over her shoulder into the pool. Before she could react, he stepped toward her and folded her into his arms, one hand roaming down her back to her backside. He laughed when her face expressed shock as her butt flexed under the pressure of his splayed palm.

"What are you doing?" Her voice raised an octave higher than usual. She looked to her right and saw the remote camera's red light come in. "C'mon, Logan, we're filming, and you're running out of time. Answer the question before Roberto comes out here with about a hundred lawyers."

His gaze lowered to her lips before he spoke. "Tell you the truth, Freddy, right now, I've completely forgotten what we were talking about."

The kiss came at her like a bird of prey—smooth, fast, powerful. In response, her heartbeat rose in a startling pounding of excitement. When he finished with the first kiss, he took another two.

"I don't like the feel of wet shoes anyway," she whispered when his lips left hers.

He smiled against her mouth. "There are more at the office."

She matched his smile with one of her own. "I guess I'm forgiven for all this?"

He ran his finger across her lips. "When you ambushed me at the office, I have to admit, I was pretty angry. I had a big project in the works and my future on the line. I didn't realize it then, but I was about to embark on an adventure that would change everything I thought I knew. These past few weeks, spending all this uninterrupted time with you, had me doing some self-discovery."

"And what did you discover?" she whispered.

He cupped her face. "That I'm more whole and more happy when you're around, and that I don't want to go on a dream vacation, any vacation, anything at all, without you."

For a minute, she thought it was raining, just like it had been the first night they spent in the mansion, but then she realized it was because she was looking at him through tears.

"But Roberto said we had to follow the script. How did you…" Her voice trailed off when he leaned over and kissed her.

"Would you please let me win this one?" he whispered against her lips.

She knew if she tried to say anything, her tears would pour. She could hardly believe what was happening. She was with the man of her dreams, and he wanted her instead of one of six of the most perfect women in the country. She looked into his incredible eyes and nodded.

"Freddy, I love you. I think it all started when you knocked me on my butt on the football field."

"It did?" She blinked, and a single tear trailed down her cheek.

"I probably didn't know it for sure then, but, thinking back, yes, that's where it began. You proved my equal, my match, first as a friend and now, as something more." He pulled her into his arms and whispered into her ear. "A whole lot more if you'll let it."

Against his chest, she could feel his heart hammering at the same insane rate as her own. She pulled back as much as he would let her. "What are you saying, Logan?"

"I'm saying that I want to be more than just your friend. I've known you almost forever, and thanks to that picture you took and this game we ended up in, I know me better, too."

He stepped back and took her hands, kissing each one before dropping to one knee.

"I want you to be my wife, my lover and…"

Was she imagining it or were Logan's eyes suddenly glassy?

"…and the mother of my children."

His voice cracked on the last word and did her in. She dropped to her knees opposite him and threw her hands around his neck. "Are you sure this is what you want?"

He stood and pulled her up with him. "I have never been so sure of anything in my life." He cupped her face again and kissed her, the kiss gentle, promising that he would never leave.

When the kiss ended, she dropped her chin, but held his gaze. "Maybe we should date for a while before we jump into marriage and having children. In all the years we've known each other, we've never dated, you know. We could, like, really have nothing in common."

He laughed and shook his head, before taking both her hands in his. "Okay then. Rikka McAllister, want to go out with me?"

She launched herself into his arms. "You called me Rikka!" Logan caught her and nodded.

She looked into the pair of eyes she wanted to look into every day from this moment on and nodded. "Maybe I'll give you a shot."

"One long overdue."

"Your own fault."

"How long am I going to have to atone for that?"

She looked up at the sky. "Fifty years or so."

"Do I need Roberto to draw up a contract?"

"Not this time."

His gaze moved slowly across her face and settled on her eyes. "I love you, Rikka."

She cupped his cheek. "Until I'm sure you're going to notice things, for a while I'm going to be pointing out that I love you, too."

Logan's smile broke wide. "And that would be just fine with me." Then he pulled her close and kissed her the way he had wanted to kiss her since that night in the kitchen during the blackout.

Behind them, someone shouted, "Cut!"

Roberto nodded in satisfaction. "And that's a wrap."

The End

Acknowledgments

Special thanks to my husband, Donald, who lets me do my thing and never complains if he has to eat takeout. Love you, baby.

And to my forever friend, Judy, who reads everything I write and always asks for more.

And not in the least, Patt, my writing soul mate, who always tells me we're going to make it someday.

About the Author

A native of Shenandoah, Pennsylvania, Kathryn Quick has been writing since the sisters of St. Casmir's Grammar School gave her ruled yellow paper and a number-two pencil. She originally planned to earn a PhD and run for president of the United States, but opted to become a writer instead. She is a past president of the New Jersey Romance Writers and a founding member of Liberty States Fiction Writers, a multigenre writers organization dedicated to furthering the craft of writing. Her novels include *'Tis the Season*, *Sapphire*, and *Daughters of the Moon*, as well as *Firebrand*, which she cowrote with Patt Mihailoff, under the pen name P. K. Eden. When she isn't writing, she works for the Somerset County government and enjoys life with her husband, Donald, their sons, and their grandchildren.

Made in the USA
Charleston, SC
06 December 2012